A WALK ON THE BEACH . . .

Lisa explained. "Carole and Stevie are my best friends. We do almost everything together. You'd love them. They're great."

Tec smiled, lighting up her world again with his dimples. "I bet I would."

"Although they might not like you, because I don't think they're very happy with me at the moment. See, Stevie had this great idea—Stevie has a lot of great ideas, only sometimes they're not actually great, but they usually turn out okay, as long as Carole and I help, but I can't help this time because I'm here and the stable is a zillion miles north. On the other hand, Stevie said Phil would help and I'm sure he'll do a better job than I would, so I shouldn't worry, and maybe Red was going to help, but I know Veronica would be useless. . . ."

Lisa realized she was blathering. She interrupted herself. "Am I talking too much?"

"Absolutely," Tec said. "And you should stop because I want to kiss you, and it's very hard to kiss a girl who's talking."

Lisa stopped talking.

the SADDLE CLUB

HORSE LOVE

BONNIE BRYANT

A SKYLARK BOOK
NEW YORK • TORONTO • LONDON • SYDNEY • AUCKLAND

Special thanks to Laura Roper of Sir "B" Farms

RL: 5, ages 009–012

HORSE LOVE
A Bantam Skylark Book / July 2000

ISBN 0-553-48697-7

Visit us on the Web! www.randomhouse.com/kids
Educators and librarians, for a variety of teaching tools, visit us at
www.randomhouse.com/teachers

Published simultaneously in the United States and Canada

PRINTED IN THE UNITED STATES OF AMERICA

OPM   10 9 8 7 6 5 4 3 2 1

1

LISA ATWOOD OPENED one eye. It was Saturday morning. One eye was all that was necessary. She glanced at her clock and her mind registered the fact that there was no rush to get up. She closed the eye again, shifted her pillow, and settled back down for a few minutes.

Not only was it Saturday, but it was also spring vacation. She had ten whole days to sleep late, spend time with her friends, ride horses, and just plain enjoy herself. Not that she didn't do some of those things when school was open, but she could do more of them this week.

Lisa reopened her eye to check the weather. It was going to be a nice day—a good day to ride. She opened the other eye. Thinking about riding made her think about wanting to get up. She was going to meet her two best friends, Carole Hanson and Stevie Lake, at Pine Hollow Stables, and the three of them were going to do something together.

Normally, Saturday meant a meeting of Horse Wise, their Pony Club; but their instructor, Max Regnery, was taking a vacation, so there wouldn't be any Pony Club for the next two weeks. They'd have their regular riding class, but there was no rush to get to it, since class wasn't until the afternoon.

Well, maybe there was a reason to hurry, just a little. Stevie had said something the night before about a project. Specifically what Stevie had said was "I have a great idea." It sometimes made Lisa nervous when Stevie made that kind of announcement. Stevie often had ideas, and some of them were great. Others, however, tended to fall into the harebrained category. A few were just downright disastrous.

Lisa, Stevie, and Carole were best friends because they were all totally horse-crazy, not because they were alike in any other way. In fact, they all knew it would be almost impossible for them to be more unalike. Stevie, for instance, had a wild imagination; she was flamboyant; she was impulsive; she was sometimes even a little weird. She was a practical joker who occasionally forgot to consider the consequences of her humorous escapades. She could be sharp-tongued with people who displeased

2

her—usually her brothers or Veronica diAngelo, Pine Hollow's chief snob-in-residence. Stevie lived life on the edge, running a little late for everything and garnering grades at school that just got her by. She sometimes said it was her teachers' fault: If they wouldn't send her to the principal's office so often, she wouldn't miss so much class time. That was what Carole and Lisa referred to as Stevian logic. It wasn't logical at all.

Stevie also had a heart of gold. She would go way out on any limb for a friend, risking *days* in the principal's office, grounding at home, and even restricted riding privileges at Pine Hollow. She had a strong sense of justice and loyalty. These were qualities that endeared her to her friends almost as much as her wacky sense of humor, and it made them willing to help her when she needed it—which she often did.

Lisa could not have been more different from Stevie. She was cool and rational, never impulsive. She planned her days and weeks well in advance so that she could accomplish all she needed to do. She never handed in a school assignment late. In contrast, Stevie had once had to explain to a teacher that the reason a lab report hadn't been completed had to do with a brother filling her pen with disappearing ink in retaliation for a phone call Stevie had made to his girlfriend, telling the girlfriend that he had bad breath.

Lisa was always neatly dressed in clean, freshly ironed clothes. Stevie's idea of clean was something that came off the *top* of her dirty laundry pile. When Stevie got herself and often her friends into a pack of trouble, she was the one who would come up with a wild scheme that might, just might, work. Lisa, with her naturally analytical mind, was the one who would come up with a sensible way to solve the problem.

Carole was as different from Stevie and Lisa as they were from each other. While all three girls were horse-crazy, Carole was the horse-craziest. She'd begun riding when she was just a toddler living on Marine Corps bases where her father, now a colonel, was stationed. She'd been devoted to ponies and horses since that first day, and one of the few things of which she was absolutely sure was that she'd be with horses all her life. She didn't know exactly what she wanted to do—be a vet, a trainer, a competitor, a breeder, or an instructor. Sometimes she thought she'd be all of those things, and then some.

She was so horse-crazy that everything else took a backseat. On a day when she had school and a riding lesson, she might leave her school backpack with books and assignments at home, but she would never, ever forget to take her riding clothes. If a horse stumbled and the rider fell off, Carole would ask someone else to look after the rider while she checked to make sure the horse was okay.

Since the girls shared a love of horses and a willingness to help one another out, they'd decided to form a club of their own and call it The Saddle Club. The only requirements for membership were those two things. The girls often extended the rule about helping one another to helping others, and that was what Stevie's great idea had been about. She hadn't elaborated, just assured Lisa it was going to be wonderful, even if it meant a little work.

Stevie's idea of "a little work" often meant a gigantic task and usually one that someone else had to do. Lisa was definitely nervous about Stevie's plan—whatever it was. She closed her eyes again.

She could hear her mother puttering in the kitchen downstairs. Actually, it wasn't really puttering. The coffeepot hit the counter a little too loudly and a glass landed in the sink with a clank.

From the hall near the door, Lisa heard her father ask, "What's going on?"

"As if you didn't know!" her mother called back.

Lisa pulled the covers over her head.

She heard her father walk down the stairs and into the kitchen. She couldn't totally muffle the conversation, nor could she hear it all. They were annoyed with one another. That had been happening quite a bit lately.

Lisa's father was traveling a lot for his job, and her mother often complained about it. Lisa didn't like to know that her parents were arguing, and she especially didn't like to get any details about the arguments from her mother. Lisa understood, though. Her mother was lonely. She loved to travel, but she had a job, and a daughter, that kept her home. Lisa's father got to travel. And even though he said that his business travel wasn't much fun, Mrs. Atwood felt left out.

And the night before at dinner, Mr. Atwood had told them that he had a business trip to Europe coming up. Mrs. Atwood had been grumbling ever since. It gave Lisa a chill.

The phone rang. The noise was loud enough to convince Lisa that she wasn't going to go back to sleep. She climbed out of bed, deciding to get dressed and go over to the stables to find out what Stevie's great idea was.

She washed up and slipped into some jeans and a shirt and a sweater, packing her riding pants, boots, and hat into her stable bag. Then she went downstairs to get some breakfast.

Her parents were sitting at the kitchen table when she got there. There was a smile on her father's face, and her mother wasn't looking grumpy at all.

"Guess what?" her mother asked.

"What?" Lisa countered.

"We're going on a trip!" said her mother.

"Oh, really? Where are you going?" Lisa asked, suspecting that her father had arranged to take her mother along on his trip to Europe.

"No, I mean *we*. All of us," her mother said.

That didn't make sense. The European trip was in the middle of her spring semester.

"*We* are?" Lisa asked.

"Yes! We're going to San Felipe."

"That's in the Caribbean, not Europe," Lisa said. One of the things she was good at was geography, and she knew that the Caribbean was nowhere near Europe.

Lisa's father could see that she was confused. "Well, your mother and I talked about this last night and decided it would be good for all of us to get away, together," her father said, emphasizing the word *together*. "So I called the travel agent, and she's found a last-minute bargain for us."

"What do you mean, 'last-minute'?" Lisa asked.

Mrs. Atwood's eyes brightened. "Tomorrow! We're leaving on a flight at eight-thirty tomorrow morning and we'll be on the beach by, well, I would say three o'clock. Does that sound about right, sweetheart?"

"It sounds about perfect, darling," he said.

"Isn't it wonderful?" Mrs. Atwood asked.

Lisa swallowed, taking the time to think. Her idea of wonderful was a week spent with her friends at Pine Hollow. Her parents could be *together* all they wanted in San Felipe, but she'd rather be with her friends. On the other hand, it had been a while since they'd taken a trip together, and her father had been doing a lot of traveling alone. Maybe it wouldn't be so bad—not that she had a choice.

"Well, I—"

"Oh, sweetie," her mother said. "Think of the palm trees and the tropical breezes and the moonlit beaches . . ."

Her mother was directing the words at her, but Lisa knew she was talking to her father. It gave her another pause for her own thoughts. Being in San Felipe would mean missing out on Stevie's great idea. Now *that* had something going for it!

"And there's so much to do! We'll have to shop and buy some resort clothes. . . ."

The idea of shopping anywhere, anytime, was enough to thrill Mrs. Atwood.

"I don't need any clothes," Lisa said. "I've got all my summer stuff."

"Well, you're going to need a new sun hat."

"I can't get that here. I'll bet they have them at the resort."

"And some sunscreen."

"They'll definitely have that on San Felipe."

"I guess they will. Well, even if you don't have to shop, I certainly do."

"The car will be here for us at five-thirty tomorrow morning," her father said.

"I'll be ready," Lisa promised him. "For now, though, I'm going over to Pine Hollow. I'll stop at the drugstore on my way back and I'll pick up some sunscreen just in case. I could use another bottle of shampoo."

"See you later, sweetie," her mother chirped.

"Bye," she said, taking a piece of toast with her on her way out the door.

Parents, Lisa thought, *are infinitely confusing*. Last night and this morning, she'd been able to feel the ice between the two of them, and now, at the ring of a phone her mother was happy and her father was hopeful.

"Hey, look who's here!" Stevie declared brightly as Lisa walked into Pine Hollow a few minutes later.

"Sleepyhead," Carole teased.

"Don't waste time making fun of her," Stevie said. "There's too much to do."

"Listen, I—"

"Yeah, right, wait until you hear what Stevie's cooked up this time," Carole said.

"Well, but I—"

"No buts," Carole said firmly. "It's a good thing you didn't wear your dressy clothes because—"

Lisa realized that she'd never be able to get a word in edgewise. The only thing she could think of was to move the conversation out of the aisle.

"Let's get into the tack room," Lisa said, shooing her friends in that direction.

"Exactly what I had in mind," said Stevie. "Did you come up with the same plan?"

"What is she talking about?" Lisa asked Carole.

"It's her great idea," said Carole.

"What is?"

"The tack room," Carole said, though her reply didn't tell Lisa anything. She was beginning to think that her friends were more confusing than her parents.

The three of them stepped into the tack room and Stevie closed the door.

"Well, what do you think?" Stevie asked.

"About what?" asked Lisa.

"Start from the beginning," Carole said.

"Oh, right," said Stevie. Starting at the beginning was not the easiest thing for her. She took a deep breath.

"Okay, so here's my idea: Max's birthday is next week, and he and Deborah have taken baby Maxi on a trip. They're going to be gone for a full week. That should give us just enough time to clean and repaint this disaster of a room." She gestured, pointing out the obvious: smudged walls with peeling paint, hooks bent askew, and drooping tack.

"He's been complaining about the condition of this place for months," Carole said.

"You're right, he has," Lisa agreed. Max was not only their riding instructor, but also the owner of Pine Hollow, and he always cared about its condition.

"Won't it be great?" Stevie asked.

Lisa nodded. It would be. And Stevie was right: It was a weeklong project for three hardworking volunteers. The bad news was that there would be only two of them, and she had to tell her friends that.

"Um," she began.

"You're not going to disagree, are you?" Stevie asked.

"No, I don't disagree. It's a perfect project and birthday present for Max. I don't disagree at all. It's worse than that, though. I can't help."

All the enthusiasm drained out of the room.

"Why not?" Carole asked.

"I won't be here," Lisa answered. Then she told her

friends about that morning's events at home. "I can't say no to my parents. They were really happy about the trip and about being together as a family."

Stevie was not one to be daunted when she was on the trail of a great idea. "Don't worry," she said. "We can do it without you."

"What do you mean, *we*?" Carole asked. "The two of us can't possibly do this alone."

"I didn't mean just the two of us," she said. "I talked to Phil last night and he was all excited about it. He said he'd help, and he told me he'd get A.J. to help, too. Those two guys together will be almost as good as one Lisa."

Lisa laughed for the first time all morning. Phil Marsten was Stevie's boyfriend, and A.J. was Phil's best friend. The two of them lived in a nearby town, and both were riders who owned their own horses. They had been talked into joining in on more than one of Stevie's great ideas before, so it didn't surprise Lisa and Carole that they'd been enlisted this time around.

"Okay, look," Stevie said, pulling a large piece of paper out of her pocket. "I've worked out this schedule." She unfolded the paper to reveal a chart. The chart broke down the task of emptying the room by setting up a temporary tack room in the feed storage room, and it included a plan for cleaning, spackling, painting, and then restocking the tack room. It broke the tasks down by half days and showed the entire job being completed by the following Sunday morning, a few hours before Max's anticipated return—and, incidentally, Lisa's return as well.

"Look, all we have to do is to take Lisa's name out and insert Phil's and A.J.'s and we're in business. We'll miss you, that's for sure, but these guys can do it. And Phil promised."

"I feel terrible," said Lisa.

"Don't," Carole told her. "Just think how nice it'll be to sit on a tropical beach while we sweat, scrape, sweep, and paint."

"That's what I mean," Lisa said.

"And it's what I mean, too," said Carole. "You've been talking about how your parents have seemed sort of crabby recently. They need a vacation and so do you. You need the time on the beach."

"And don't worry," Stevie said. "When you get back, we'll have lots and lots of things for you to do to make up for all the work you missed this week."

"I guess that's what I'm afraid of," Lisa said. "The manure pile?"

"It'll be waiting for you," Stevie assured her.

"Well, then, maybe it's okay if I go."

Just then, the door to the tack room flew open. The

girls didn't even have to look to see who it was. There was only one person at Pine Hollow who would not respect a closed door with at least a knock.

"Come on in, Veronica," Carole said without turning.

Veronica diAngelo sashayed into the room as if she owned it, looking disdainfully at The Saddle Club.

"Have you rented the place for the day?" she asked.

"No," Stevie told her. "We were just planning. We're going to paint this room as a birthday present for Max. Would you like to help?"

Stevie, of course, knew what the answer would be. She just wanted to give Veronica the opportunity to utter her favorite phrase.

"Isn't that what stable hands are for?" Veronica asked. She picked up her horse's tack and walked back out of the room without another word.

The girls waited until Veronica was around the corner before they began laughing. It was strangely comforting to have someone so completely predictable in their midst.

"I still wish I could be here this week," Lisa said when the girls calmed down.

"Don't worry. We both wish we could be in San Felipe," Stevie assured her.

"I guess that makes us even," Lisa said, smiling. "And

I can't even help you begin the pre-paint cleanup. I've got to go get some sunscreen, shampoo, and boring stuff like that before I pack. I'm out of here."

The girls hugged one another. Lisa promised to send postcards, which they all knew would arrive about a week after she got home.

As she walked out of the room, Lisa could hear Stevie flipping open her chart.

"All right, now, the first item is moving everything."

"Then let's get started," Carole said.

Lisa smiled. She definitely had mixed feelings about missing out on this great idea, but the beaches of San Felipe seemed like a good alternative.

LISA FUMBLED WITH the key card to her cabin. She slid it in one way and it didn't work. She turned it around. Still no luck. She turned it over. The little light turned green and the door swung open.

Glancing around, Lisa realized it was a nice cabin—not too fancy, but just right. It had a single bed in it, nighttable, dresser, mirror, clean bathroom. It was all she needed, really, but it seemed kind of empty. She wished, not for the first time that day, that she had a friend with her.

The trip to San Felipe had been uneventful. The plane was full of vacationers, all traveling in pairs or as part of groups, headed to the islands in search of sun. Lisa had suddenly felt lonely. It didn't help that, since

16

their reservations had been made so late, her seat was far from her parents'. She'd sat with a young couple, apparently on their honeymoon, who seemed totally uninterested in talking to Lisa except when they had to climb over her to get to the lavatory.

When they'd arrived at the resort, she'd found the same held true for their rooms. Her parents' cabin was in one section of the resort and hers was in another. It didn't really matter. Lisa was old enough not to need her parents next door, but she did feel isolated, as she had on the plane. The one piece of good news was that the honeymooners were nowhere in sight.

Well, the first few minutes or hours in any new place are always a little awkward, Lisa told herself. *The thing to do is to be logical.* Lisa was good at being logical, and she knew what the logical thing to do was now: She unpacked. It took her all of five minutes. It only took another five to shed her spring clothes from Virginia and put on a pair of shorts and a T-shirt with some sandals.

The next step was to see what her parents were up to. Lisa tucked her key card in her pocket and set off in search of their cabin.

Her parents were nowhere near as logical as Lisa. Their suitcases weren't unpacked, and they hadn't even changed their clothes.

When Lisa asked what they should do first, her

mother told her that they were both tired and were planning to take a nap. Lisa could do whatever she liked, but if she didn't want to nap, how about going for a swim?

"We'll see you at dinner. Seven o'clock in the dining room, okay?" her mother suggested.

"Okay," she agreed, though it didn't feel okay, and it particularly didn't feel okay when the door to her parents' room closed. What it felt was lonely.

On the other hand, Lisa realized that her parents had been up even earlier than she had and that they were both probably tired and they also needed time together. *Okay*, she told herself. *I'll go for a swim*. After all, the ocean was there, it was warm, it was inviting, and she had enough sunscreen to last three vacations.

She returned to her room, put on her bathing suit, picked up her sunscreen, book, two towels, hat, and sunglasses, and headed for the beach.

It was late afternoon when she got there—late by resort standards. Most of the vacationers had gotten their fill of sun and fresh air and were back in their rooms showering and getting ready for the evening. Lisa welcomed the quiet. She spread her beach towel out on the sand, slathered herself with sunscreen, and then lay down, tucking the other towel under her head for a pillow. It was all she needed. Almost as soon as she closed her eyes, she was asleep, her mind filled with visions of scraping and sweeping, washing and painting, and mounds of tack piled in the middle of her room at the resort.

"JUST WHAT IS going on here?" Mrs. Reg asked, looking at the large pile of tack that Stevie and Carole had made in the middle of the feed room. Mrs. Reg—short for Mrs. Regnery—was Max's mother and the stable manager. Her hands were on her hips and there was a scowl on her face. Mrs. Reg did not tolerate a mess in her stable.

"We're moving the tack room stuff," Stevie said.

"I can see that. What I want to know is, why?"

"For Max," Stevie began.

"I hardly think he'll thank you for making a mess in the feed room," she said.

"No," Carole said, "you don't understand—"

"You've got that right," said Mrs. Reg.

"It's Max's birthday present."

"Well, he *will* be surprised . . . ," she said sarcastically.

"I think I'd better explain," Stevie said. Those were the words Mrs. Reg was apparently waiting to hear, and she listened patiently as Stevie told her about her great idea for Max's birthday surprise.

As Stevie showed her the chart and explained their schedule and their full plan, Mrs. Reg's scowl turned into a smile.

"Oh, Max is going to love it!" she said. "But where's Lisa? Isn't she going to help you?"

"Lisa's on some Caribbean island," Stevie said.

"San Felipe," Carole supplied.

"But Phil's going to help instead," said Stevie.

"Well, let me rephrase my question, then," said Mrs. Reg. "Where's Phil?"

"May I use your phone?" Stevie asked.

She followed Mrs. Reg back to her office and picked up the phone, dialing a number she knew well.

Mrs. Marsten answered and told Stevie that Phil was at A.J.'s house and she might just be able to catch him. Stevie hung up quickly and dialed A.J.'s number.

A.J.'s father answered the phone. "I think they're still here," he said. "Hold on a sec."

Stevie could hear him calling the boys' names.

"Just caught them," he told Stevie a few seconds later. "Phil will be right here."

Stevie figured the two of them were on their way over to Pine Hollow, and that would be good news for them—as well as for Mrs. Reg.

"Hi, beautiful! I've been meaning to call you. It's a

good thing you caught us because we were on our way out the door!"

"How long until you get here?" Stevie asked.

"Where?" he asked.

"Pine Hollow," she said, suspecting she was not going to like what she was about to hear.

"Actually," said Phil, "A.J. and I are on our way to Vermont. His aunt has a condo at a ski resort, and she has room for the two of us for the whole week!"

"Phil!"

"Isn't that great?"

"What about the tack room at Pine Hollow?" she asked.

"What about it?" he answered, his head apparently in a snow-induced fog.

"Remember how you said you'd help with painting the tack room while Max is away?"

"We'll be back next week. We can help you then."

"It's going to be done by then!" Stevie said.

"Great!" he said. "Listen, I promise I'll be thinking of you as I'm flying down the mountains. Vermont has wonderful skiing, you know. It's some of the best in the world. I got these skis for Christmas and I haven't even had a chance . . ."

"Phil!"

"What's the matter?" he asked, finally realizing that

Stevie was not exactly excited for him. "It's just painting. You can do that without me."

"You promised me," she said. "And Lisa can't be here, so we really need your help."

"Look, Stevie, I'm sorry, but this just came up and when the snow is fresh, you can't say no. Um, A.J.'s mom is taking us to the airport. I've got to go. I'll send you a postcard, okay? Bye, sweetie. I'll miss you!" As Phil hung up the phone, she could hear him calling out, "Okay, okay, I'm coming!"

She hoped he'd miss his plane.

"Stevie?" Mrs. Reg said rather curiously. Stevie knew she'd heard enough of the conversation to know that Phil wasn't coming. Phil's words stung, but so did the doubtful look on Mrs. Reg's face.

"It's okay, Mrs. Reg. We'll get it done."

"It's a big job," Mrs. Reg said.

"It's just painting," Stevie said, echoing Phil's remark. "We can do that without Phil."

"And Lisa?"

"Of course," Stevie said, though she didn't really feel that way.

"Stevie, perhaps you should reconsider . . . ," Mrs. Reg began.

Those were the words she needed to hear. All it ever took to convince Stevie she absolutely had to

22

do something was somebody doubting that she could do it.

"Oh, no problem," she said. "In fact, the last time Phil so-called helped me with something, it took twice as long. Carole and I will have this well done before Max and Deborah get back. Actually, we might even paint the grain storage room, too."

"Uh, that's not necessary," said Mrs. Reg. "The tack room will be just fine, thank you."

"You're welcome," Stevie said. By this time in the conversation, Stevie was more than a little numb. She'd just promised Mrs. Reg that she and Carole were going to finish a project she hadn't been at all sure she, Carole, Lisa, Phil, and A.J. could have done in a week. Was she out of her mind?

Carole was waiting for her when she returned to the feed room.

"Look," Carole said. "I think we can move this bin out to the shed for the week. It's got the winter feed in it and we're about done with that, and that'll make enough room for some temporary saddle racks, and then the bridles can go over here. It'll mean taking the bridle hooks off the walls and moving them in here temporarily, but we'd want to do that to paint, anyway, wouldn't we?"

Stevie didn't have the heart to tell her right then that

they were going to be working alone. She just listened to Carole's suggestions, and when Carole was done, she nodded and said, "Let's get started."

It wasn't until the last saddle was moved out that she had the strength to share her news.

"We'll do the best we can" was all Carole said. Stevie hoped that would be enough.

LISA COULD FEEL herself breaking into a sweat. The sandpaper block felt heavy in her hand. Up, down; up, down. Layers and layers of paint merged into one another, forming a cloud of dust that billowed everywhere. It glared brightly through the dark afternoon sunlight in the stable. It settled on her clothes and her skin, penetrating her T-shirt, gritty, dry. She breathed in, filling her lungs with dust.

It tickled her nostrils, teasing her sinuses. And there was more, still gritty and dry.

"*Ah-ah-ahhhhh-choooo!*" She sat bolt upright.

"God bless you!" said an unfamiliar male voice.

Lisa looked up. The bright sun was glaring. She was outdoors, not in the stable. And she could hear the gentle rush of surf, not the scratch of sandpaper. It took a second, but she realized she wasn't at Pine Hollow—wasn't even in Virginia. She was on San Felipe, and she'd fallen asleep on the beach, dreaming about the work she was missing at the stable. What had made her sneeze was nothing less than the silky soft sand on which she'd been taking a nap.

"Thank you," she said, brushing off the sand.

"You're welcome," said the voice.

Lisa shaded her eyes to see who was blessing her.

"Tec Morrison, at your service," he said.

"Oh, hello. I'm, uh—what's your name again?" she asked, instantly wishing the dumb question hadn't come out of her mouth.

"Tec. It's short for Tecumseh. See, my parents had this passion for American history. What do your parents have a passion for?"

"Huh?" Lisa asked.

"I mean, what's your name?" he asked.

"Oh, Lisa. I think they just liked the name. Lisa Atwood."

"Glad to meet you, Lisa Atwood," he said, offering his hand.

She took it and he held hers tightly while he helped her stand up.

As soon as she was standing and looking straight

at Tec Morrison, Lisa began wondering if she'd be able to stay standing, because her knees were starting to buckle.

"Whoa, there," Tec said. "You must still be half-asleep." He steadied her with his other hand.

"And maybe still dreaming," she said, hoping at once that he hadn't heard her. But he had and he seemed pleased.

"Nah, it's just the tropical sun. And if you think it's strong, wait until you see what the tropical moon does!"

Her eyes took in the entire person standing in front of her and she knew at once that she wouldn't have to wait to find out the effects of the tropical moon. There was nothing in the world that could have changed her entire view of all existence as quickly and as totally as one good look at Tec Morrison. And she also knew that any look at Tec Morrison was a good look.

He was about six inches taller than Lisa and wore a yellow boxer-style bathing suit that perfectly showed off his luscious tan, which, in turn, showed off his taut, muscular torso. His face was almost heart-shaped because of the widow's peak in his sun-bleached light brown hair. His blue-gray eyes smiled warmly, melting Lisa's heart almost as much as his slightly crooked grin, which was punctuated by boyish dimples.

Lisa gulped.

"Moon?" she asked.

"Well, it should be up before too long," he said. He raised one eyebrow questioningly, almost as if he were issuing an invitation.

But the idea of moonrise suggested to Lisa that she'd been asleep rather longer than she'd expected. "What time is it?" she asked.

Tec shrugged. "Time isn't very important around here," he said. "Maybe six-thirty, I guess."

"Oh," Lisa said. "I've got to go. I'm meeting someone—um, I mean, my parents told me to be in the dining room at seven."

"Then I guess you'd better go, unless you want to wear that bathing suit in the dining room, and, since it would surely distract all the diners there as much as it's distracting me, I strongly suggest you change first. Goodbye until the moon rises," he said.

And with that, he leaned over and picked up her towels, her beach bag, and her book and handed them to her. Then, almost before she could thank him, he ran off down the beach toward one of the sections of resort cabins.

Lisa's feet were pinned to the sand, watching his receding form. Food? Clothes? What did they matter when there would be moonlight soon—when there were blue-gray eyes and dimples?

28

She sneezed again and a breeze from the ocean gave her a slight chill. Evening was coming. So was seven o'clock. She wrapped her sandy towel around herself and set off in search of her cabin, a shower, and some clean clothes.

While she showered and dressed, Lisa found herself wondering how much of what she remembered at the beach was real. She knew she hadn't been sanding at Pine Hollow, but was that boy real? Could someone that beautiful really exist? *Tec. Tecumseh. Tecumseh Morrison.*

Lisa tried to remember what she could about the Shawnee chief after whom Tec's parents had named him. He'd been a noble warrior and a fine leader. He had believed that the land belonged to all of the tribes and therefore it was impossible for the European Americans to acquire territory by war or even by trade. The tribes could not cede what was not theirs. She'd remembered liking that idea when she'd learned it in school. And now she knew why she liked it so much. Blue-gray eyes and dimples.

Lisa looked over the selection of dresses she'd brought with dismay. Back in Virginia, they'd seemed like a perfectly nice selection of summer dresses, and until she'd met Tec, she'd still felt that way. Now that she *had* met Tecumseh Morrison, however, she was sure they were all totally girlish. Too pretty, too frilly, too . . . well, too much like the old Lisa might dress, not the Lisa that had met Tec Morrison.

But they were all she had. She finally picked out a blue one—simply because it was neither pink nor yellow—slipped into a pair of delicate white sandals, added some simple gold hoop earrings, and looked at the result in the mirror. Not bad. At least, not too bad. If only she could be three years older and ten years more sophisticated. But she couldn't. And besides, Tec seemed to like her just the way she was. The trouble with that was that he didn't know her at all. And what he wanted was to see her in the moonlight.

Lisa's stomach fluttered and she had no idea how she would ever manage to eat anything. The one thing she did know, however, was that she would be in a whole lot of hot water if she didn't meet up with her parents, but fast.

She looked at her watch. It was already ten after seven. She put on a light coat of lip gloss, smiled at herself in the mirror, and headed out the door.

The dining room was in the center of the resort. Her room was in a cluster of cabins on one side of the place; her parents' room was in a cluster on the opposite side. There were no phones in the rooms, so there had been no way for Lisa to tell her parents that she was running late. By now, though, she was just plain running. Her parents weren't particularly understanding of lateness.

Lisa found there was a short line to get into the dining room. They'd stayed at a similar resort before, and she knew that the hostess would seat people at tables as they came in. Most of the tables were large, holding about eight people, and in order to encourage people to meet new friends, the guests were expected to eat with whoever was in line with them.

Lisa glanced over the shoulders of the people in front of her, looking for her parents. She didn't have to look very far. They were at a table close to the door, and they were sitting at one of the rare tables for two.

"Hi, sweetie!" Her mother waved to her cheerfully. "We'll see you after dinner, okay?"

Lisa sighed. If only she'd known. She could have soaked in the shower a good deal longer! And now she was faced with the prospect of eating by herself or with a whole group of strangers. It didn't make her feel any better. She found herself looking forward to the day when her parents would start behaving normally again.

"One," she said to the hostess.

"Make that two," said someone behind her.

Lisa turned. It was Tec.

"What luck!" he said to her.

He doesn't know the half of it, Lisa thought.

The hostess led the two of them over to a table where there were six other people. Later on, Lisa realized that she couldn't have identified the other people at the table if her life depended on it. The only person she saw was Tec Morrison.

Together, they looked over the buffet. Lisa took a plate and made herself put some food on it, although she knew she had no appetite whatsoever. Tec piled his plate high.

"You don't know what you're missing!" he said. "But don't worry, I'll let you taste some of my goodies and then you can go get some yourself."

"I think my appetite got ruined on the airplane this morning," said Lisa.

Tec laughed. "Airplane food is the worst!" He held her chair for her while she sat down. "Did you have a long flight?"

"From Washington—uh, D.C.," she said.

"Really? Do you live in Virginia?"

"I do. I live in Willow Creek. Do you live there, too?" she asked.

He told Lisa the town and she'd heard of it. It was about seventy-five miles from Willow Creek. There were fifty states in the country, and it turned out that the most attractive boy in all fifty of them lived in the very same state that she did. Was there a more perfect world anywhere?

"When did you get here?" Lisa asked.

"Two days ago, and we're staying until Tuesday."

"Just Tuesday?" she asked. Maybe the world wasn't so perfect.

"I mean a week from Tuesday," he corrected himself.

He would be there every single day that she was. And he'd be there after she left, too. But two days later, he'd be back in Virginia. Lisa's mind raced. Seventy-five miles was a long distance, but at least it wasn't 750 miles. Stevie had a boyfriend who lived ten miles away and they managed to work it out and stay together. She and Tec would find a way, she was sure.

"I'll be here until next Sunday," Lisa said. "I have to go back to school that Tuesday. You have a really long spring vacation, huh?"

"It's worked out pretty well," he conceded.

"So, tell me, since you've been here so much longer than I have, what's fun to do around here?"

"With you? Almost anything," Tec said.

Lisa's heart skipped a beat. Two, maybe three, she thought. Tec wanted to spend time with her. She wanted to spend time with him. She put her fork down. There was no way she could eat another bite.

"Lisa, honey!" It was her mother. "There you are!"

"Hi, Mom."

Her mother looked at Tec. "It's nice that you're making friends, dear," she said rather expectantly.

"Mom, I'd like you to meet Tec Morrison. Tec, this is my mother, Mrs. Atwood."

Tec stood up and took Mrs. Atwood's hand. "Pleased to meet you."

Mrs. Atwood glowed. She loved good manners, and Lisa knew that Tec had just earned himself a whole stack of points by standing up and shaking her hand.

"Well, sweetie, your dad and I are going to have an after-dinner drink in the lounge and then we're going to the show. Will we see you both there?" she asked.

What an awkward question, Lisa thought. It was as if her mother wanted to know if she and Tec would be together later, and much as Lisa suspected and hoped that they would be, she wasn't about to jump to any conclusions. At least not out loud.

"I'm not sure what we'll be doing, Mrs. Atwood," Tec said, answering for Lisa. "I'm sure we'll see you later, though."

"I'll look forward to that," Mrs. Atwood said, smiling back at Tec. "Have fun, sweetie," she said, and then she left them, heading for the lounge with Lisa's father.

"I, uh—"

"Don't say a word," said Tec.

Lisa looked at him, wondering what he meant.

He answered her unasked question. "I've got parents, too," he said. And she got it.

There was a moment of quiet understanding. Then Tec spoke again. "Look, since you pigged out so badly on dinner, how about you try a few of the desserts here. I'm telling you, the cheesecake is really great. Want me to bring you some?"

"That'd be good," said Lisa. "A really small piece," she added.

"I'll bring you a big one and I'll eat whatever you don't," he said.

"Deal," she said.

Lisa looked across the room, trying to take in the crowd while Tec maneuvered through the throng and fetched them two large plates of cheesecake. The room was full. Everywhere she glanced, people with various levels of tans and relaxed looks seemed busy, happy, full, and content. Lisa was sure, though, that none of them was as happy as she was that night.

Tec was right about the cheesecake. It was very good, but she could only eat a few bites. Tec was true to his word. While they talked about all the activities they could do the next morning, he finished off the considerable remains on her plate.

And when he was finished with that, he did something that totally surprised her. He reached under the tablecloth and took her hand. She felt a shiver of pleasure pass through her.

"And now that we've decided what we're going to do tomorrow, let's talk about what we'll do tonight. I heard a rumor that there's a nearly full moon. We could go down to the beach and look at the reflection on the water. Would you like to do that?"

"Yes," Lisa whispered. She was sure that was the loudest noise she could make at that very moment. "Yes," she said again.

"OUCH!" STEVIE SAID.

"What?" asked Carole.

"I pinched my hand." Stevie was trying to set one of the heavier saddles down on a sawhorse in the feed room and had managed to trap her hand against the raw wood. Carole lifted the saddle enough for Stevie to pull her hand out.

"It's nothing," Stevie said, shrugging.

"It's a bruise," Carole corrected her, pointing to the mild swelling that was beginning to show on the back of Stevie's hand.

"Nothing," Stevie repeated.

"It's not nothing if that's your painting hand," Carole said.

"I'm a totally ambidextrous painter," Stevie assured her.

The two of them returned to the tack room to move the next batch of saddles and bridles.

They had been working for hours. It didn't really surprise either of them that Stevie was getting a little careless. What did surprise them was what Stevie saw when she looked out the window.

It was dark out there, but the sky was filled with stars and a beautiful nearly full moon. "Check that out!" Stevie said, pointing to the sky.

Carole leaned over to see out the dusty window of the tack room (soon to be washed *and* freshly painted). The sight nearly took her breath away. "It's so big and it's not even full yet. It's like it's sitting just above the horizon. . . ."

"It's that pretty orange-gold color, almost as if it's been toasted," Stevie said.

"I like it when it's not quite full," Carole said. "It has a sort of lopsidedness to it, like it's not perfect but will be."

"You mean, like it's got promise?" Stevie asked.

"Exactly," Carole said. "But speaking of promises, we've got one to work on."

Stevie shook her head in dismay. The fact that it was night and the moon was up meant that they'd been working even longer than she'd thought, and it was beginning to seem like they would be working forever.

"I think maybe this was a bad idea," Stevie said.

"No, just a big one," Carole told her, handing her a box of bits. "Look, we're getting tired. Why don't we quit for the night and pick up where we left off tomorrow?"

"But it's just a few more loads."

"It's not a few more loads, it's a lot more loads," Carole said sensibly. "And they'll still be here tomorrow. By then, we'll be a little more rested."

"And we will have eaten," Stevie said. Food was not often far from her mind.

"Yes, that, too," said Carole.

They took the last load of the night into the feed room and rearranged some of the grain bins.

"That's it. It's time to go home," said Carole, slinging her arm across Stevie's tired shoulders.

Stevie stood up and followed Carole out of the room and along the aisle to the door of the stable.

"It's really time to murder Phil Marsten," Stevie said. "If he'd stuck to his promise, we'd have had everything moved by now."

"And if Lisa had been here, too, it definitely would've been done," Carole agreed. She zipped up her windbreaker against the chill of the spring evening. "And if pigs had wings—"

"But he promised," Stevie whined.

"Hey, think of it this way," Carole said. "You're forever telling me there's nothing Phil does that you can't do as well."

"True, but I didn't say he'd do this any *better* than I can. I just said we need his help. And instead, he's skiing a zillion miles away."

"And Lisa's on a beach a zillion miles in the other direction."

"Oh, she's not on a beach at this hour of the night!" Stevie said.

THE SOFT, WARM waves tugged at Lisa's bare feet. The receding water pulled away sand, making Lisa feel as if she were sinking. But if she was sinking, so was Tec, because he was standing right next to her, still holding her hand. He hadn't let go of it since they'd left the dining room, and Lisa found herself hoping he never would.

" . . . and then yesterday morning, they told me we were going on a vacation. It's like it was . . . I don't know, fate," she said. "Yesterday, I thought it was a strange idea. Now, well . . ." Her words hung, the rest unspoken, unnecessary.

"My parents planned this for months," Tec said. "It

was a Christmas present, but I've known about it since August."

"Well, it's a nice place," she said.

"Yeah," he agreed. They splashed along the beach where the tide lapped at the sand.

They had been walking and talking for two hours. The moon, once an orange platter near the horizon, was now a nearly round silver plate high in the blue velvet sky, attended by thousands of stars. Lisa felt more alive than she had ever felt in her life. It was as if she could feel, see, hear, smell, and taste the entire world around her. The salt sea smell mingled with the sweet scent of Tec's aftershave. The tropical breeze caressed her shoulders—except where her arm touched his. The stars and moon seemed to reflect in his eyes and off his tanned skin, making him glow. And inside, Lisa felt a similar glow warming her.

They talked, and they listened to each other, too. Everything about Tec, everything he told her about himself, everything he said about her, all seemed right, balanced, true. Although they'd known each other for only a few hours, Lisa was beginning to think that their souls had known each other forever—that they were almost one.

"What would you be doing now if you were home?" Tec asked.

"That's easy," Lisa said. "I'd be with Stevie and Carole."

He frowned ever so slightly. "Who's Stevie?" he asked. "A boyfriend?"

It took Lisa a second to understand what he was asking, because it had been so long since she'd thought of *Stevie* as a boy's name. "Short for Stephanie," she explained. "Those two are my best friends. We do almost everything together. You'd love them. They're great."

He smiled, lighting up her world again. "I bet I would."

"Although they might not like you, because I don't think they're very happy with me at the moment. See, Stevie had this great idea—Stevie has a lot of great ideas, only sometimes they're not actually great, but they usually turn out okay, as long as Carole and I help, but I can't help this time because I'm here and the stable is a zillion miles north. On the other hand, Stevie said Phil would help and I'm sure he'll do a better job than I would, so I shouldn't worry, and maybe Red is going to help, but I know Veronica would be useless. . . ."

Lisa realized she was blathering, but she couldn't help it. The very thought of her friends trying to finish an enormous project without her had reminded her of the fact that part of her thought she ought to be in Virginia.

She interrupted herself. "Am I talking too much?"

"Absolutely," Tec said. "And you should stop because I want to kiss you, and it's very hard to kiss a girl who's talking."

Lisa stopped talking.

Tec took a small step toward her and pulled her to him. Still holding her right hand with his left, he put his right hand on her shoulder and slid it around her back, drawing her closer still. Then he leaned down, looking uncertainly into her eyes. Lisa couldn't help smiling at him. All uncertainty left his face. He smiled back. And then, as their lips met, she closed her eyes. All her senses became one, and they all focused on Tec Morrison.

Lisa had no idea how long they stood there, locked in that kiss. Even later, she couldn't have said if it had been four seconds or an hour. It seemed an eternity, and it changed everything.

And then they walked along the beach in pleasant silence for a while. Soon, they began talking again.

"So," Lisa said. "What would you be doing if you were home now?"

"I think I'd be working on my lines," Tec said.

"Lines?"

"A play. I'm in the spring play at the high school. I'm Artful Dodger."

"In *Oliver!?*" she asked.

"Right. You know the play?"

"Well, I've seen it done. But I've never been in it. The last play I was in was *Annie*."

"You starred, I bet."

It was true. She had. "Well . . ."

"I can see you with a shaved head, playing Daddy Warbucks."

Lisa laughed. "That's my part!" He smiled at her. Oh, those dimples! "It was just community theater," she said. "But it was fun. I really loved it."

"I do, too," Tec said. "The way an audience reacts when you do it right for them—it's like a drug."

"I never thought of it that way," said Lisa. "I just love the music and dancing—you know, the smell of the greasepaint. The whole thing. Isn't it cool that we both love the same thing?"

"It just seems right," he said, squeezing her hand.

"I guess we have a lot in common. I don't suppose you ride horses, do you?"

"It's the next thing on my list to take lessons in," said Tec.

"Really?"

"Really," he said.

"Well, you know they've got a stable here. I've signed up for a trail ride tomorrow. Would you like to come along? I could teach you."

"That would be great. What time?"

"How about eight o'clock?" she suggested. "The trail ride leaves at eight-forty-five."

Tec glanced at his watch, which made Lisa look at hers. She couldn't believe her eyes. It was after one o'clock in the morning! She and Tec had been walking and talking—and kissing—for over five hours, and she could have sworn it was little more than half an hour. The time had simply flown.

"Could we make that eight-thirty?" he asked. "I think I could make it by then, but I'm not positive."

"Sure," she said. "I'll meet you at the stable then, if you can make it and if we don't see each other at breakfast first."

"What would I need to wear?" he asked.

She told him that he'd need long pants and some shoes with a heel. "See, if you don't have a heel on your shoes, you run the risk of having your foot slip through the stirrup, and that can be really bad. They probably have hard hats, so you don't have to worry about that. I guess it's already pretty warm here by eight-thirty in the morning, so you won't need a jacket. They'll have riding crops, too, and you can probably choose between English and Western. If you're a totally new rider, Western may be better for you because the saddle is easier to sit in and, even though it's bad form, you can hold on to the pommel if you need to."

"That's what the rope goes on?"

"Yes, on a Western saddle. All modern pleasure riding saddles have evolved from working saddles. The English saddle we use today is a cousin of the saddles that were used on battlefields in the past. They are light so that the horse doesn't have to carry any extra weight. The Western saddle is more substantial, because a cowboy could have to be sitting in it for eight or ten hours at a time. It's a seat, a sofa, a desk, a workspace. Sorry," she said, stopping herself.

"What?" Tec asked.

"I'm beginning to sound like Carole."

"Well, Carole must be very smart."

"She is," Lisa said. "Except that she doesn't always know when to stop explaining things about horses."

Tec laughed. "I think I'd like your friends," he said.

"You will," Lisa promised him. "But right now, if I don't get some sleep, I'm not going to be good at explaining anything when we go on that ride."

"I take it that's a cue," Tec teased.

"It is," Lisa said.

They walked to her room. In the moon-shadowed darkness of the tropical evening, Tec kissed her, then disappeared into the night.

Lisa sighed and opened the door to her cabin. It took only a few seconds to get ready for bed. As soon as her head hit the pillow, she realized there was far too much to think about for her to be able to sleep. Her mind was a jumble of thoughts. Actually, there was only one thought: Tec Morrison.

"OUCH!" STEVIE SAT upright in bed to massage the aching, overworked muscles in her right shoulder. If they hurt now, they were going to hurt a lot more the next day after hours of cleaning, scraping, and painting.

"Phil Marsten, I hate you!" she said, punching her pillow—with her left fist—for emphasis. She shifted to her left side and put her head back on the fluffed pillow. She was asleep in a matter of seconds.

AT SEVEN-THIRTY the next morning, when she was brushing her teeth, Lisa was barely aware that she'd had only a couple hours of sleep. Who needed sleep? And who wanted sleep when there were people to spend time with and hold hands with and . . .

She sighed, splattering toothpaste on the counter. It wasn't easy brushing her teeth when she couldn't erase the gigantic grin on her face, because that made it hard to reach her back teeth.

It would have to do. She spat and rinsed, wiping the counter as she did so. Then she took a moment to look at the girl in the mirror. She was pretty sure it was the same girl she'd seen there before—the one she'd seen every morning of her life. She was still Lisa, but there was something palpably different about her. Was it the smile? Maybe. The little bit of color she'd gotten the day before from the sun? Perhaps. But there was something else: a maturity, a wisdom, a mere feeling. Who knew? And it didn't matter, except that it made all the difference in the world. She'd met Tec.

She hadn't expected to meet Tec. She couldn't have guessed she'd meet him or that he'd meet her, but they'd met and they'd held hands and talked and walked and then kissed and nothing in the whole world was ever going to be the same. Sure there was a smile, a glow, but the only part that mattered was what was inside, and that was the part that held thoughts of Tec.

Lisa ran a comb through her hair, slipped into her riding pants and boots, pulled on a polo shirt, found her gloves and riding hat, and then left the room, closing the door behind her.

She was going to breakfast. Tec *might* be there. And then she was going to the stable. Tec *would* be there. They'd ride together and she'd teach him, but she reminded herself that she didn't want to be too bossy or talk too much about riding. She just wanted to enjoy his company and tell him enough to be safe. He wasn't preparing for a show or anything, so keeping his heels down, toes in, and elbows firm wasn't going to matter anywhere near as much as staying on the horse!

She smiled, knowing herself too well.

The dining room was buzzing and full. She paused at the door, looking for Tec, but there was no sign of him. She did, however, see her parents. They were at a table with a couple of empty seats, and they waved at her to join them. There would be room for Tec when he arrived. She picked up a glass of orange juice and a dish of fruit and sat down.

"Nothing ever changes, does it?" her mother teased. Lisa had no idea what she was talking about, because it seemed to her that everything in the world had recently changed.

"Your riding clothes," her mother explained. "You've already found the stable?"

"Oh, right, that," said Lisa. "Yes, I thought I'd go for a trail ride. It's best if you do that in the morning before it gets really hot."

"I'm glad they've got horses here," her father said. "Makes me feel less guilty about dragging you away from your stable on vacation."

"You don't have to feel guilty," Lisa said, smiling. "I like it here already."

"So do I," said her mother.

"Me too," said Mr. Atwood.

Lisa finished her dish of fruit and glanced at her

watch. It was 8:15 and time to get going. "I'll see you guys later."

"We're going on a snorkeling picnic," her mother said. "It leaves at ten-thirty and will be back this afternoon. Want to come along?"

Lisa didn't want to miss a minute of her possible time with Tec. "No thanks," she said. "I think I'll still be at the stable then. I'll get along by myself. See you this afternoon, then, or at dinner in any case."

"Have a nice ride," her mother said.

"I will," Lisa promised, leaving them with a wave and a smile.

All the way over to the stable, Lisa kept looking around for Tec. He should be walking over there now if he was going to be there by eight-thirty—though Lisa didn't know where his cabin was and didn't know from which direction he'd be coming. Maybe he was there already. It would make sense for a new rider to get to the stable early, even if it meant skipping breakfast, to get to know his horse. Even as an experienced rider, Lisa might have thought of doing that herself. She chided herself for wasting time on a bowl of fruit.

"Hi. Are you joining the trail ride?" a young man asked her. He looked at his list. "You must be Lisa Atwood?"

"Guilty as charged," said Lisa. "Actually, I think there will be two of us. Has Tec Morrison signed up yet?"

The man checked his list. "Nope," he said, shaking his head. "Nobody by that name. And the ride is full, so I hope he's not expecting to go out with us today."

"Oh," said Lisa. It hadn't occurred to her that the list would fill up. Tec might be annoyed with her for making him get up so early for nothing. Maybe she should give him her place.

But he wasn't there yet, and Lisa was. When he showed up, they could figure out what was the right thing to do. In the meantime, Lisa proceeded as if she were choosing a horse for him.

"Just something easy and reliable," she said.

"Okay," said the man, who had introduced himself as Frank. "You haven't ridden much?"

"Um, well, just for a while," she said.

Frank looked at her a little oddly and she knew why. Her riding pants, though clean, were clearly used, and her boots were well broken in. It was true that she hadn't been riding all that long—not compared to Stevie and Carole—but it wasn't true that she was inexperienced. What Frank thought didn't matter, though. What mattered was that Tec got a horse he could handle.

Frank brought out a horse he introduced to Lisa as Oatmeal and then began bringing out the tack. Without thinking, Lisa began tacking up the horse. At Pine Hollow, riders were expected to tack up their own horses, and it was completely automatic for Lisa to do so now—especially when her mind was foggy with fatigue. She slid the saddle into place and began buckling the girth and adjusting the stirrups expertly.

"I wish all my beginners were as knowledgeable," Frank teased. Lisa smiled, realizing what she'd done.

"Well, I just—"

"Don't worry," he said. "I'm glad for the help. Can you do the bridle?"

"I guess so," she said, accepting it from him and then sliding it over Oatmeal's head, slipping the bit into his mouth.

"Okay. Riders? Are we all ready?"

Lisa looked around her, noticing the others for the first time. There were four other riders, plus Frank, a group of six all together. The others were patiently standing by their horses. With Frank's signal, they began to mount.

There was a young couple—newlyweds, Lisa thought—who seemed as new at riding as they were at being married. The wife began by trying to get on the horse from the wrong side. Her husband started to help her, but in doing so, he dropped the reins to his own horse.

Lisa wrapped Oatmeal's reins around a fence post and went to give them help, holding the husband's horse's reins while instructing the wife on how to get her boot into the stirrup. Then she showed the woman how to hold her reins, while the husband looked on. Lisa hoped he'd learned something, but when he went to mount, he wasn't much better. She explained patiently that putting his foot into that side of the stirrup would result in a twisted stirrup leather—unless he wanted to sit on the horse backward.

He thanked her for her help, listened carefully, followed instructions, and was soon in his saddle, facing the right way, with his reins held properly.

Frank had been busy helping an elderly gentleman who seemed to know what he was doing, but who needed to use the mounting block because of what he called "these creaky old bones."

The other rider was a young woman whom Lisa thought she'd seen in the dining room the night before. She was wearing a staff shirt for the resort, but she didn't seem to be a stable worker, though she clearly knew what she was doing on a horse.

Frank mounted his horse and lined them up. Frank asked Jane—the staff member—if she could lead the way since she knew the trail. Next came Lisa, then the older man, and then the honeymooners, followed by

Frank. Lisa understood the lineup perfectly. Jane was a good rider, so he wanted her in the lead, but the best rider always had to be at the back to keep his eye on the riders who might most easily get into trouble: the honeymooners. He'd clearly figured out that Lisa was a better rider than she'd told him, and he knew the old man knew what he was doing on a horse, creaky old bones and all.

Lisa was still looking for Tec as they began their ride out of the stable area, but there was no sign of him. It was almost nine o'clock. He'd definitely overslept.

Lisa shrugged as Oatmeal followed Jane's horse dutifully. Vacations were for sleeping, she reminded herself. A big boy like Tec probably needed a lot of sleep. She shouldn't have kept him up so late the night before, and she promised herself she wouldn't do that again. They'd part at a reasonable hour so that he'd have a better chance of coming along on the next day's trail ride.

Jane began to trot as they reached an open area near the beach. Oatmeal seemed content with his gentle walk. Lisa nudged him. No response. Lisa nudged again, more firmly. A little grudgingly, Oatmeal picked up a trot. It was annoying to ride a horse who was so nonresponsive, but Lisa realized she'd asked for it when she'd told Frank she was a new rider. Maybe it wasn't such a bad thing. She was scouting out the horses for Tec, and

Oatmeal might be just the one for him. This was a horse who would never get into any trouble. Oatmeal was slow, plodding, and agreeable. He wasn't going to win any races, unless they were against turtles.

Tomorrow. It was not only her favorite song from *Annie*, it was also what she couldn't stop thinking about, because tomorrow Tec would be riding with her. Lisa decided she was glad he hadn't come this morning. It gave her a real opportunity to spend time thinking about the lesson she wanted to give him when he was there the next day.

She'd tell him the basic stuff he'd need to know: sitting up straight, looking in the direction he wanted to go. (She'd learned early on that horses were very sensitive to their riders' balance, and if a rider gawked in one direction, the horse was likely to turn that way without any other signal.) She'd tell him how to hold the reins and show him the difference between neck-reining as Western riders did it and opening reins the way English riders did it. She could tell him a million things, but that would be a mistake. She knew that for sure.

"Lisa!"

It was a sharp warning call. Lisa halted automatically.

"What?" she asked, surprised to find Frank riding next to her.

"You've got to pay attention!" he said. "You're heading straight for that gully!"

Lisa looked where he pointed. She'd let Oatmeal wander to the right of the line of the trail, and they were aimed at a steep dip that would be a challenge to any horse but might be deadly to an obedient plodder like Oatmeal.

"I'm so sorry," she said. "I was thinking—"

"You weren't thinking," Frank said sternly. "But you have to. I can tell you know better than that."

"I do," she said meekly.

"Well, stop daydreaming then and pay attention."

"Yes sir," she said.

She *was* tired. She was really too sleepy to be doing anything that required attention, but her near accident had served to wake her up. She knew she probably wouldn't have gotten hurt if Oatmeal had slid down that embankment, but Oatmeal might have, and that was inexcusable. She knew better and she'd do better.

She sat up straight and focused on the trail in front of her.

The trail led the riders through a stand of palm trees and then onto the beach. Jane's horse began to trot, and on the firm, water-cooled sand, even Oatmeal seemed pleased to strut his stuff. Lisa found herself enjoying the wind and the sweet sound of her horse's hooves slushing through the Caribbean waters.

Jane let her horse drop back so that she and Lisa were riding abreast.

"Isn't it wonderful?" she asked.

"The best!" Lisa agreed.

"Canter?"

"Do you think this old guy can do it?" Lisa asked.

"We'll just see," said Jane, sliding her foot back to signal her horse to a canter.

Oatmeal had it in him. Lisa felt the delightful transition as Oatmeal shifted from a two-beat trot to the three beats of a canter. She settled into her saddle and simply took pleasure in the wonderful feeling of it all.

She always enjoyed cantering. At Pine Hollow, she and her friends often cantered in the ring and in the paddocks around the barn. There were even places on the wooded trails where the terrain was open enough and smooth enough to canter, and it was a pleasure. But cantering on the beach was a very special pleasure, with the bright sun above and the sparkling blue ocean and the knowledge that there was a wonderful boy waiting for her when the ride was over. In fact, he was bound to be embarrassed about missing their date and had probably left a message for her at the stable already. Lisa took a deep breath, knowing that Tec was not far away and was breathing the same tropical air that was entrancing her.

In front of her, Jane brought her horse to a trot and then a walk as the beach narrowed. Oatmeal followed suit without any instruction from Lisa. The other riders, none of whom had joined in the canter, were far behind. Lisa pulled Oatmeal up next to Jane's horse.

"That was great!" she said.

"It always is," Jane agreed. "Um, say, did I hear you singing earlier?"

"Me?"

" 'Tomorrow,' I think it was."

"I guess so," Lisa admitted sheepishly. "I didn't even realize I was doing it out loud. I'm sorry."

"Don't be sorry," Jane said. "It's earned you the right to skip the chorus audition."

"Huh?"

"I'm in charge of the talent show," she explained.

"I didn't know there was one," said Lisa.

"Only when we've got talent—and I think we do, based on what I heard earlier."

"Oh, thanks. Well, I have done a little community theater," Lisa admitted.

"It's a lucky community," Jane said. "Anyway, I could let you know what the rehearsal schedule is this afternoon, if you're interested." Lisa nodded. "Great! I don't suppose there are any more like you at home?" she teased.

"Well, my parents don't really sing much, but there is someone . . ."

Tec. Artful Dodger was a challenging part. He'd be perfect in the resort talent show. They could work together on something they both loved. Maybe they could even sing a duet. She could wear—

"Who is it?" Jane asked, interrupting.

"Oh, it's a guy I was talking with last night. He's been doing musical theater, too."

Jane's face lit up. "Hey, let's put on a show!" she said. She and Lisa shook hands.

Jane clucked and nudged her horse into a trot then, leading the line back away from the beach and through a hilly area that would return them to the stable. The ride was over, but Lisa knew it was the beginning of another exciting adventure. With Tec.

When they returned to the stable, Lisa was relieved that the resort didn't follow Pine Hollow's rules that required riders to untack and groom their own horses. For once, she was almost eager to leave. She had to find Tec—who had not left her a message at the stable—but she didn't want to run into him until she'd had a chance to shower. She was hot and sweaty and smelled a little more like Oatmeal—the horse, not the breakfast—than most boys would find attractive, unless they *really* loved horses.

By eleven o'clock, Lisa was clean and freshly shampooed, had put on her bathing suit, cover-up, sun hat, and all the sunscreen she'd need and headed to the beach for a swim. As if by a magnet, she was drawn to the place where Tec had kissed her the night before—the place where everything had changed in an instant.

He wasn't there.

She walked along the beach, carrying her towel, hoping to find him, but there was no sign of him. It had seemed so logical that he'd be where they'd been; that he'd be drawn back there just as she was. But he wasn't.

She kept walking, her eyes scanning the swimmers and sunbathers. *Maybe he went on the snorkeling trip*, she thought. The idea that he'd spend the day with her parents did not comfort her at all. Lisa climbed the concrete steps by the basketball court to the small pool where a rowdy, happy group was playing water polo. Between the water polo pool and the large swimming pool, there was a long row of beach chairs, and there, stretched out on one of them, sound asleep, was Tec Morrison.

Being as quiet as she could so as not to wake him, she spread her towel out on the empty chair beside Tec and lay down on it. She closed her eyes, and fatigue overcame her in a matter of minutes. She slept soundly until the water polo ball bounced off her stomach and onto Tec's legs. That was enough to rouse both of them.

"Ouch!"

"What the . . . ?"

Tec stared at her in surprise, his confusion compounded by the apologetic cries from the water polo players.

"Sorry," Lisa said. "It bounced off me."

"Oh," he said. Then he let himself sink back down onto his seat.

"Good morning."

"I don't think so," Tec said. "I definitely have not slept enough yet."

"You missed a good trail ride," she told him.

"What?"

"We were going to go horseback riding this morning, remember? I guess you slept through it, but that's okay. Anyway, it was fun and you're going to love it tomorrow."

"Oh, right," he said. "I forgot."

"That's all right," she said. "And now I've got some even more exciting news for you."

"What's that?" he asked.

"There's a talent show on Saturday night, and we're

going to be in it. Isn't that cool? A sort of 'Annie Meets the Artful Dodger.' Do you like the idea?"

"You have been busy this morning," he remarked, smiling at her.

"Very," she agreed. "And now I'm ready for a swim. How about you?" She stood up, eyeing the inviting pool in front of her.

"You show me first," he said. "And I promise to save you if you start drowning."

Lisa dived into the deep end of the pool while Tec settled back onto his lounge chair. The next time Lisa checked, his eyes were shut and he was asleep. That was good. He was going to need rest.

"MRS. REG!" LORRAINE Olsen wailed. "Look what Carole and Stevie have done!"

Stevie cringed. Carole fumed. Mrs. Reg appeared. She frowned, but she stood up for them.

"They're doing something useful," Mrs. Reg said.

"Not for me, they aren't!" Lorraine snapped. "I can't find anything. Where's my saddle?"

"Is that what you want?" Stevie asked, sounding much more polite than she felt.

"Of course it's what I want," Lorraine answered, sounding ruder than Stevie thought absolutely necessary.

"Well, then you might have told us, because everything that has been moved out of the tack room is in a perfectly logical order," Stevie said, just a tiny bit unsure what the logic was and stalling for time. "See, all the saddles that were on the right-hand wall are on the, um . . ."

"Mine was on the left," Lorraine said.

"Well, then, but left walking in or out?" Stevie asked.

"Left walking in," Lorraine told her.

"Well, because there isn't really a left wall in this room, since the door is on the extreme left, we put all those saddles by the feed bins—"

"Stevie, this room has feed bins everywhere," Mrs. Reg said. There was an edge to her voice that told Stevie she'd better have an answer fast.

"Well, then, you see, here—" Stevie suddenly remembered the system and her face and voice brightened up considerably. "It's on this sawhorse, on the *left* side of the biggest bins. See? There is a system!"

"And my bridle?"

"Carole can help you with that," Stevie said, turning the floor over to her partner in grime.

Not that Stevie was off the hook. Right behind Lorraine was April and then Betsy. Last but not least for that morning's lesson was Veronica diAngelo. Actually, it wasn't Veronica. She'd sent Red O'Malley, who spotted Veronica's tack immediately and took it without bothering Stevie and Carole. He also spotted and fetched Betsy's tack.

It took Stevie and Carole almost as much time and effort to locate and deliver the riders' tack as it had to move it all in there the day before. They strongly suspected that when the tack was returned, it would not be in the strict order that they'd devised (even if they couldn't always remember what the order was), but that was a problem for another hour.

Things quieted down between the tack and feed rooms when the class started, and Carole was ready to get back to their job. Stevie, however, was distracted.

"I'm just going to kill him," she said.

"Who?" Carole asked, alarmed.

"Phil Marsten."

Carole sighed. She was also annoyed that Phil had decided skiing was more fun than painting the tack room, but if she had a choice, she'd be on the snowy slopes right now, too.

Carole sat down on a bale of hay, next to where Stevie was perched on a sack of grain.

"I think we need a break," Carole said.

"We need to take advantage of a moment of quiet to get back to work," said Stevie.

"We've been working hard for two hours already this

morning," Carole reminded her. "You know what they say about all work and no play?"

"No, what do they say?" Stevie asked.

"It makes Stevie a very grumpy girl," Carole said.

"Well, maybe Stevie's got a good reason to be grumpy."

"Sure, but she'd have a better reason to be cheery if she took a nice trail ride."

"Do you think that would be okay?" Stevie asked.

"I think Belle would be grateful for the opportunity to get out in the fresh air and have a sip of some cool water from Willow Creek."

"Hmmm. I wonder if I can find her saddle."

"It's a very simple system," Carole said. "If it was on the right-hand side of the tack room, then it's on the back wall, either on the sawhorse or perched on top of the winter feed, in alphabetical order by the first name of the rider who usually rides the horse or by the horse's middle initial, if the horse is a predominantly American breed. If the horse is a European breed, then it's alphabetical by the second letter of the owner's last name, unless the owner is Pine Hollow, in which case it's numerical in reverse order by height of the horse with the exception of horses whose manes naturally fall on the right as opposed to the left side of the neck or horses who have leg markings on an even number of legs."

Stevie giggled. The system they'd worked out wasn't *exactly* as complicated as Carole was making it sound, but it hadn't been easy to devise a system that would work for the transition.

"Oh, I remember! The real basis of the system was that our own saddles would be the easiest to reach," Stevie said, standing up and taking her own tack from the nearest surface. "Now *that's* a totally logical system!"

"I definitely agree with that!" said Carole, taking her saddle from next to where Stevie's had been.

"Meet you by the good-luck horseshoe in, um, six minutes," Stevie said, glancing at her watch.

Six minutes later, the girls mounted their horses and brushed the horseshoe, which was by the stable door. Max's grandfather had nailed it to that wall many years before, and one of Pine Hollow's most treasured traditions was that every rider had to touch it before they began any ride. The result was that no rider had ever been seriously injured at Pine Hollow. People liked to think that the horseshoe had magical good-luck qualities. More experienced riders realized that the very act of touching the shoe reminded them to be careful because what they were about to do could be dangerous.

Carole and Stevie were pleased to find that, unlike their impression from the dusty stable, it was really a lovely spring day, fresh and warm, with bright sunshine gleaming its promise down on the last wintry strains of the season.

Carole took a deep breath, invigorated by the combined scents of fresh air, horses, and leather.

"Wonderful!" she declared, bringing Starlight to a trot.

Stevie and Belle followed suit. Stevie could feel herself healing in every way as they proceeded through the paddock to the woods.

There was no question where they were headed. They were going to the creek—The Saddle Club's own special spot. It wasn't as if nobody else knew about it, but they all thought that nobody else got as much fun out of it as they did.

Carole led the way, walking, trotting, and cantering as the paths allowed. They knew exactly where they were going and exactly how to get there. With each step, their horses seemed to awaken from their own winter haze, and their gaits became more lively as they approached the spot by the creek that they all knew so well.

Carole drew Starlight to a halt and dismounted. Stevie did the same with Belle. They let their horses have a drink from the creek and then secured them to a bush where there were some fresh sprouts of spring grass to munch on. Since Belle was allergic to certain kinds of weeds, Stevie was always super-careful about where she secured her, but she knew that this was a safe spot. The horses immediately began munching—resulting in a sound of utter contentment.

"This way, my friend," Carole teased, leading Stevie to the rock where the friends always sat.

It wasn't summer yet, but the girls had both removed their sweaters and tied them around their waists. A cotton shirt was all that anyone needed today. Stevie sat on the rock and then scooted forward, reaching for the water. Willow Creek began in a nearby mountain, and sometimes in spring the water felt more like the ice it might have been not long before than it did water; but today, the water was relatively warm. That was all the invitation Stevie needed. In a matter of seconds, she and Carole had both removed their boots and their socks and were dangling their weary feet in the healing waters of Willow Creek.

"It's almost summer," Carole said, wiggling her toes against the chill of the rushing water.

"I agree with the *almost*," Stevie said, withdrawing her feet for a few seconds. "Except that I've got a whole bunch of school left."

"But now is vacation, so let's focus on that," said Carole.

"It's a working vacation, that's for sure," said Stevie.

"And I'm beginning to suspect we've bitten off more than we can chew—especially without Phil."

"And Lisa," Carole reminded her. "If you aren't mad at Lisa for going away with her parents, how come you're so mad at Phil for going away with A.J.?"

"Are you asking me to be logical?" Stevie said.

Carole laughed. "I guess I am making that terrible mistake," she teased. "But I've been thinking. We are trying to do something nice for Max, and if it takes longer than the time he'll be away, well, then it will. No matter when it gets done, it'll still be a nice thing we did for Max and a real birthday surprise for him."

Stevie didn't answer right away. She dangled her feet again and wiggled her toes. She was still inclined to be angry with Phil. "But everything's such a mess," she said.

"So it's a little disorganized. People will get used to it. They can see what we're up to and they'll go along with it."

"Mrs. Reg is annoyed at us."

Carole shook her head. "I don't think so," she said. "I think she's pleased that we're doing the job and that she doesn't have to do anything for it. I think she wishes it would get done faster, but she knows what we're up against. Mrs. Reg is never angry when people want to work at Pine Hollow, remember?"

"But we won't have any time for any fun on our vacation!" Stevie said.

"This is fun, isn't it?"

Her logic was compelling.

"Look," Carole said. "We're doing our best, which is all Max ever asks for."

"That sounds reasonable," Stevie conceded. "But I hate to think of the mess those riders from today's class will leave when they put their saddles back."

"So, then they'll have more trouble finding their saddles next time," Carole said.

"You're so calm about it all!" Stevie said.

"What choice do we have?" Carole said with the kind of logic that Lisa usually applied to problems.

Stevie laughed. "Okay, okay, I give in," she said. "We'll just get as much done as we reasonably can without killing ourselves."

"Or anybody else," Carole said.

"Not even Phil?" Stevie asked.

"Not even Phil," said Carole, and she knew they'd struck a deal.

"You know what I think?" Stevie asked, looking into the clear waters of the creek.

"What?" Carole asked.

"I think loving a boy is complicated," she said.

"I guess," said Carole, though she hadn't had as much

experience with boys as Stevie had. "Loving horses is simpler," Carole said.

"Definitely," Stevie agreed. "And besides, they never go skiing."

Carole and Stevie laughed a little, then sat in contented quiet.

After a while, both girls took their feet out of the water, lay back on the rock, and gazed up at the blue spring sky, visible through the still-bare branches of winter.

"DID YOU SEE that yellow fish?" Lisa asked, removing the snorkel from her mouth.

"I did—and there was a school of blue ones, too. Did you see them?"

"I sure did," she said. "They almost seem to glow, the blue is so bright!"

"Well, the sight of all that food, pretty as it is, has made me hungry," Tec said.

"And I have just the cure for that," Lisa told him.

The two of them were snorkeling at a coral reef off a small beach at the edge of the resort. There were only a few other swimmers and picnickers there, and Lisa felt almost as if they were in a world of their own.

When they'd both awakened from their poolside naps, they'd made a deal: Lisa was in charge of making a picnic, and Tec was in charge of getting snorkeling equipment. Neither job was hard. The resort was only too happy to have visitors use their facilities, and sandwiches, chips, and sodas were packed into a cooler in a matter of minutes. Tec got their flippers, masks, and snorkels as easily, accompanied by directions to the beach and then to the small coral reef.

They swam back to the beach, removing their snorkeling equipment as the water became shallower. Then they dried off and settled down on towels in the sand to enjoy the lunch and to continue doing what the two of them did so well: talking. It seemed to Lisa that there was nothing she couldn't say to Tec and nothing he wouldn't share with her. How could it be that they'd met each other less than twenty-four hours before? Already it felt like a lifetime—a wonderful lifetime.

"Turkey or tuna?" she asked.

"How did you know those were my two favorites?" he asked.

She'd just known.

STEVIE AND CAROLE drew their horses to a halt in the ring by the stable's double doors and dismounted. They were both glad for the break they'd taken. Now they felt ready to continue their job, no matter how long it took, and Carole was convinced that Stevie's anger had dissolved a little in Willow Creek. That would definitely make it easier to work with her.

They walked their horses to their stalls, untacked them, and then took the equipment back to the grain storage area.

"What's this?" Stevie asked, entering first.

Carole was dismayed. She guessed that Stevie had been right about everybody making a super mess when they'd returned their tack after class.

"Bad?" Carole asked.

"I don't think so," said Stevie.

"We saved your places over there," Carole heard Lorraine tell Stevie. She stepped into the room to see what was going on.

What had before been half filled with tack was now completely filled with tack. Anna McWhirter showed up at the door on the other side of the room, holding a large cardboard box.

"That's the last of it," she said.

"Good," said Lorraine. "Because we're now completely out of space here, unless we want to stop feeding the horses."

"What's going on?" Carole asked.

"We're helping," said Lorraine.

"I can see that," said Stevie. "But what inspired you?"

"You didn't tell us this was a surprise for Max," said

Anna. "There's no way it'll get done before he gets back without help from everybody."

"Will someone please tell Red where to put my saddle!" Veronica diAngelo demanded, pushing her way into the room.

"Almost everybody," Anna corrected herself.

Veronica disappeared as quickly as she could.

"Okay, so now the tack room is empty. I figure the next step is the best cleaning it's ever had," said Lorraine.

"Just what we had in mind," Carole agreed.

"I've got the broom," said Anna, holding it high.

"And I've got the bucket," said Betsy.

"I think the mop is in the bathroom," said April.

Stevie turned to Carole. "Well, what are we waiting for?" she asked.

"I'll get the cleanser while you find the spackle," Carole said.

"BOY, I'M READY for a good long nap now and I bet you are, too," said Tec, holding Lisa's hand outside her cabin door.

"I am," she said, smiling back at him.

"I'll come knock on your door for dinner at eight tonight, okay?"

"It's a date," she said.

"And you get all the rest you can before then, because there's going to be dancing in the disco tonight and I want to be sure you're up to it."

"I will be," she promised.

He leaned over and gave her a quick kiss. "Sleep tight," he said.

Lisa was sure she would. It was only the middle of the

afternoon, but she'd already had a trail ride, a swim in the pool, and a snorkeling picnic on the beach with Tec. Rest was something she could definitely use—especially after being up so late the night before!

She unlocked her door and went in, aware that Tec was walking away, toward his own room.

As she stepped in, she noticed a piece of paper on the floor. She leaned over to pick it up. It was a note from Jane.

"Rehearsal 3–5 in theater," it read.

Lisa had forgotten all about the talent show and the rehearsal schedule that Jane had promised to provide. She hadn't really thought it possible that the first rehearsal would be that afternoon, but since the show was going to be on Saturday and this was Monday, there wasn't a lot of time to spare.

The problem was that although she'd mentioned the show to Tec, she'd never told him that Jane had promised a rehearsal schedule, and since she hadn't known herself what the schedule would be, there was no way he would know to be in the theater at three.

It was already two-thirty, so there was no time to waste. She had to tell him right away.

She put her key card back in her pocket, slipped her sandals back on her feet, and hurried out the door.

First she thought Tec might be in sight. It had only

been a matter of seconds since he'd kissed her good-bye, but there was no sign of him. His room was in another area of the resort, and she knew the number because he'd had to give it for identification when they'd returned the snorkeling equipment.

She hurried over to his section, still hoping to spot him on his way. It took a few minutes to locate his cabin. She was uncomfortable knocking at his door, but she had no choice. Time was passing, and she had to get to the rehearsal, but she'd need to shower and change first.

She listened at the door. There was no sound. Perhaps he was asleep already. That wouldn't surprise her. She raised her hand and knocked.

There was no answer. She waited a few seconds and then knocked again. He was a pretty sound sleeper, as she knew from watching him at the pool. She almost wished she had a water polo ball to wake him with. She knocked a third time. There was still no answer.

Either he was totally zonked, in which case he'd be too tired for the rehearsal, or he was in the shower. If that was the case, then all she had to do was to let him know what was happening. She took the paper Jane had left for her, folded it, and slid it under Tec's door. He might get there late, but he'd get there.

Satisfied, she returned to her own room for a very quick shower and changed into clean, dry clothes.

By a few minutes to three, she was racing through the open-air lounge area to the theater.

The lounge area abutted the swimming pools where she'd met up with Tec that morning. She glanced over at the seats, wondering who was occupying them now and if they were enjoying being there as much as she and Tec had.

The seats were empty, though each had a towel draped on it. Lisa turned her attention to the theater, but something caught her eye. At first she thought it was Tec, but it was hard to tell because there was a big splash fight going on.

She looked again. It wasn't Tec. It couldn't be. For one thing, Tec was taking a shower or a nap. For another, that boy was with another girl—a skinny thing, wearing a string bikini, and they were splashing one another in the pool. Tec wouldn't be with another girl, and he'd told her that he didn't like to swim in freshwater pools. It was funny to think that there would be two boys at the same resort who had similar looks—what good news for the girls who hadn't been lucky enough to meet Tec first!

Then she turned her attention to the theater and, following the clear signs, went right on in.

The rehearsal had already started. Jane waved Lisa in and straight onto the stage.

"Okay, now, chorus line, let's see how you can kick!"

Lisa put her arm around the waist of the woman next to her and, without missing a beat, joined in on the kick line. She'd certainly had enough ballet and tap lessons over the years to be able to manage that.

"Nice work, Lisa!" Jane said.

The PA was blasting a poor rendition of "There's No Business Like Show Business," leading Lisa to assume, correctly as it turned out, that they were working on the grand finale. That was one of the things she loved about putting a show together. Sometimes there appeared to be little or no logic to the order.

However, as Lisa looked around, she knew exactly what the logic was. There were almost no men present. Since a kick line was all women, it made complete sense to begin with that.

Jane had them go over the steps four or five times until it was roughly passable.

"We don't need this to be too professional," Jane said. "Enthusiasm is much more important than precision!"

Lisa smiled to herself. That was typically the case with amateur shows. The fact was that precision was impossible, so enthusiasm was essential.

Once they had the finale down, Jane checked her clipboard for other acts to rehearse.

She shook her head. "We need men," she said.

"I've got one coming," Lisa promised.

"Where is he now?"

"Taking a nap," Lisa said. "But he's got talent and I can fill him in on stuff so he'll be up to speed tomorrow. I mean, I don't think he can do the kick line. . . ."

"I don't expect that—just that he can hold a tune and is willing to sing with the chorus."

"You can count on that," Lisa promised.

"Okay, leave a space for him," said Jane, indicating where the group should make room for one more.

Jane had worked up a number of funny skits for the performers to put together. One of them was about a honeymooning couple who didn't notice anything else going on around them. It was very funny, and Lisa could easily imagine herself and Tec playing the parts—for real—but Jane wouldn't cast anyone who wasn't there.

There was a skit making fun of the activity director, and another that involved a barnyard and required several people to share costumes for horses and cows. Lisa's favorite skit was about snorkeling. Almost all of the skits required a chorus of some sort, and in each case Lisa made a space for Tec. None of this was hard. All of the music for the chorus parts was recorded, so the chorus had to do little more than be there and lip-sync. Tec could do that, for sure.

Lisa had had the foresight to stick a notepad in her pocket. As Jane described the blocking for each skit, she made notes for herself and for Tec. Since there would only be three rehearsals before the dress rehearsal, Tec would have to work hard to catch up. He could do it, though, she was sure.

"Okay," Jane said, inviting them all to sit down on stools on the stage. "Those are the general skits, and since we do variations of them with every group of guests at the resort, I can assure you the audiences love them—especially the all-male *Swan Lake* takeoff. The other part of the show will be individual performances by guests. If there are people who would like to perform, sing, dance, juggle, twirl batons, whatever, they should see me. I'll be holding auditions tonight at six and tomorrow at four. Thanks for all your good work, and I'll see everybody tomorrow afternoon, same time, same place."

Individual performances. Maybe that included duets. Could she and Tec do something? There were a lot of wonderful Broadway show duets they could sing, like "Anything You Can Do" from *Annie Get Your Gun*. Or maybe something like "Let's Call the Whole Thing Off." Either one of those would be great. They'd be showstoppers. They'd be wonderful! She knew it would be unbelievably fun to work with Tec on a silly song like that, but she also knew, and was less eager to admit, that it would be a way of showing him her talent. She didn't like to think of herself as a show-off or think that she had anything to prove, but it *would* be nice to show Tec that she wasn't exaggerating. She'd talk with him about it tonight and they could practice together tomorrow. It might not be exactly like a picnic on an almost-deserted beach, but it would mean being together and working together. She got excited just thinking about it.

"Okay, that's it. Rehearsal's over. See you next time!" Jane said. "And Lisa, I guess I'll see you tomorrow morning on the trail ride, right?"

"Of course," Lisa said. "I wouldn't miss it."

She wouldn't—and she had no intention of letting Tec miss it, either.

Lisa hopped down off the stage and headed back out into the bright tropical sunlight. It was just after five o'clock, and the afternoon seemed even hotter than it had before. She became aware of her overall exhaustion, recalling the nap she'd promised herself for the afternoon, now mostly gone. She was expecting to see Tec at eight. That gave her two and a half hours to rest and a half hour to freshen up and change before he came to pick her up for dinner. She glanced at the pool as she walked past it, wondering if she would see the guy who reminded her of Tec, but there was no sign of him or the skinny girl in the skimpy bikini.

"She probably got a terrible sunburn," Lisa told herself, and then realized she was being unnecessarily mean. She needed a nap.

8

"I THINK THERE'S a way to do this on the computer, but I don't know what it is," said Carole, glaring at a sheet of paper. What she held in her hand was a list of names. It seemed like everyone in the stable wanted to help with the painting, and that was good news. It also seemed like they all had different schedules.

"Why don't we just tell everybody to come whenever they can?" Stevie asked.

"Because then we'd end up with fourteen people in a room that can hold only four. Anyway, we only have six paintbrushes."

"And two cans of paint."

"That, too," Carole agreed. "So you had this bright idea to ask everybody when they had time. Some of them wrote times they were available; others just said when they were busy. I think if we look at this carefully, we can figure out Dr. Faisal's entire schedule for the week."

Dr. Faisal seemed to be everybody's orthodontist, and apparently every single rider at Pine Hollow was getting his or her braces tightened during school vacation.

"Well, his office is between school and the stable," Stevie reminded her.

"I know. It's just funny to see it on this paper. Now, how do we organize?" Carole asked.

"We think what Lisa would do," said Stevie.

"Ah, yes," said Carole.

Stevie perched on the desk next to where Carole had placed the sheet of paper. The two of them studied it for a while.

"Okay, first we have to reorganize this list," said Carole.

"Just what I was going to say."

Stevie pulled a fresh sheet of paper out of the desk drawer, turned it sideways, and made six columns. The first one was NAMES and the rest were the days of the week, Tuesday to Saturday. Then she broke the days into thirds and called those MORNING, MIDDAY, and AFTERNOON. This was for them to work out who was available at which times. Once they knew that, they could then begin to assign times on a second sheet of paper.

"This is just what Lisa would do," Carole said, beaming.

"Sure," Stevie agreed. "But she'd know how to do it on the computer."

Carole shook her head. "I don't think so," she said. "Lisa's not all that hot with the computer. It's Phil who could figure out how to do it on a computer."

Stevie looked at the handmade chart and smiled. "Computers? Who needs 'em? Not me!"

LISA'S EYES FLUTTERED open. She was aware of little more than the total darkness of her room. At first, she wasn't even aware of what room it was, but then the soft breeze coming through the light cotton curtain reminded her she was on vacation, at a resort on San Felipe, and that she was falling in love with the most amazing boy she'd ever met.

Then she looked at the clock on her bedside table. It was almost nine! She only had a few minutes to get to the dining room before they stopped serving dinner. She leaped out of bed, brushed her teeth, ran a comb through her hair, and pulled on a white cotton dress. She grabbed her key card, slipped into some sandals, and was out the door and onto the path to the dining room before she remembered that Tec had promised to pick her up for dinner at eight. Had she been sleeping so soundly that she'd missed him? How embarrassing!

She still felt the vague disorientation of a sound sleep when she arrived at the dining room. The line was dwindling and they were clearly getting ready to stop seating people, but she was in time . . . to have dinner with whom?

She stood on her tiptoes and looked around the place for Tec. She spotted him quickly. He was at a table full of other kids around their age. He waved to her cheerfully.

She slid past the hostess and went over to the table but was disappointed to find that there weren't any empty seats. It might not matter anyway, because it was clear they were almost finished eating.

"I guess I must have been sound asleep when you knocked," she said.

Tec looked slightly confused and then embarrassed. "Oh, no, I'm sorry," he said. "I didn't wake up until after eight, and I figured you'd already be here by then, so I came straight over."

That made sense. "Oh, good, because I was so sound asleep—well, you can't imagine," she said. "Look, I've got a lot to tell you," she began.

"Then let's get together after dinner, okay?" he asked.

"Okay," she said.

He turned to the other people at the table. "Hey, guys, this is Lisa Altman—"

"Atwood," she corrected automatically.

"Sorry. Atwood. Anyway, she'll meet us in the lounge after she's eaten, okay?"

"Great," said one guy. "I'm Will."

Lisa nodded as the others introduced themselves, too, a sea of names she was sure to forget until she got to know the owners of those names better—Kiki, Sophie, Grant, Brian, Meredith, and Alex.

"We'll see you over there, okay?" Tec said. He smiled warmly at her, once again showing those dimples that melted her knees.

"I won't be long," she promised.

"Take your time," said Kiki. "We wouldn't want you to get indigestion!"

A couple of the kids laughed and so did Lisa, though she didn't really think that Kiki had said anything particularly funny.

Lisa returned to where the hostess was taking care of the last diners, but before she was relegated to the tail of the line, she spotted her parents. They were sitting together at a table that was almost empty. Her father saw her and waved her over to them.

It seemed like days since she'd seen them. She remembered that they'd been on an official snorkeling picnic, unlike the impromptu one that she and Tec had devised. Perhaps they could compare notes.

Lisa picked up a plate and walked through the buffet, selecting a light meal—sure to save her from indigestion—and then sat down next to her father.

Over the last few months, she'd gotten very good at taking a barometric reading of her parents' moods, and she could sense right away that the mood was good. It seemed that the vacation was having exactly the effect her parents had hoped for.

"How's it going, sweetie?" her father asked. "It looks like you've made some friends."

"I guess," Lisa said. She wasn't thrilled with the idea of talking with her parents about Tec at this point. "Well, there are a lot of kids around my age here now. I guess it's because it's spring vacation for a lot of schools. Say, how was that snorkeling thing you did today?"

It was a good question to ask at a time when she didn't want to answer questions herself. It turned out her parents had had a great time.

"The colors on those fish!" her mother said.

"And you wouldn't believe the coral," added her father. "It's made entirely of very tiny animals who've colonized over many centuries. These creatures work together . . ."

Lisa was amused in spite of herself. Her mother, a natural stylist, whether it was decorating a room or planning a wardrobe, had tuned right in to the colors of the fish. Her father, an engineer, was all keen to study the construction of a coral reef. Actually, it was quite wonderful that they'd found something that had interesting aspects for each of them, no matter how different those aspects were.

Before Lisa knew it, her mother had switched subjects to talking about how good the fresh seafood salad had been at their picnic, while her father talked about watching the way the schools of fish (no matter what color) worked so that each member of the school was a lookout for one part, thus protecting the entire group from predators.

"And this afternoon, after the picnic, we went into the town. It's so charming!" her mother said.

"But your mother didn't buy a thing!" Mr. Atwood said.

"I did, too, Richard," she said.

"I don't consider that little wooden salad bowl a serious purchase by your standards, Eleanor," he teased. Instead of cringing when her father talked about her spending habits, Lisa's mother laughed. She didn't mind being teased the way she minded being nagged.

"Well, your father ignored three phone calls from

the office!" Mrs. Atwood said, smiling proudly at her husband.

"I didn't exactly *ignore* them," said Mr. Atwood. "I just called back and told them to solve the problem themselves."

"Which means you didn't climb on a plane to go take care of it personally," said Mrs. Atwood.

"No, dear. I'm on vacation."

Mrs. Atwood leaned over and gave him a little kiss on the cheek. It wasn't much, but Lisa knew the whole performance had been for her benefit. This was her parents' way of telling her that they knew things had been difficult all around over the last few months and that they were better now and would stay that way.

Lisa took a bite of the seafood salad she'd put on her plate. If it was the same as what her parents had had on their picnic, her mother was right: It was delicious.

"So what did you do today?" her father asked.

"Oh, I've had a busy day," Lisa said.

"Well, you were going riding when we saw you at breakfast," said her mother.

Lisa smiled. Breakfast seemed so long ago.

"We had a trail ride. We went along the beach. It was wonderful!"

"Did you have a good horse?" her mother asked. It was quite typical of her mother to ask something like

that, though by "good" her mother didn't mean obedient, well-mannered, and with smooth gaits. What her
mother meant was "valuable" or "good-looking." Lisa
had yet to find a way to convince her how unimportant
those things were in a pleasure-riding horse.

"Very good," said Lisa.

"I'm surprised in a public stable at a resort," said Mrs.
Atwood.

"His name is Oatmeal," Lisa said.

"Soft and warm," said her father.

Lisa laughed. "Exactly," she said. "And quite sweet,
too."

"Wholesome?" he asked.

"A little too wholesome," she said. "Tomorrow, I'm
going for something with a little more spirit."

"Sounds like you were being a bit conservative," said
her father.

"It's always been my downfall," said Lisa.

"And is that how you met all those nice young people?" her mother asked.

"On the ride? Oh, no," said Lisa. "I just met them
tonight," she said.

"Well, wasn't that the boy—"

She really didn't want to talk about him now, especially when she knew he was waiting for her in the
lounge. Any discussion that centered around a boy Lisa

had met was going to include a barrage of questions about what his father did for a living and what he was going to be when he grew up, and Lisa couldn't and didn't want to answer.

"There were just a few people on the trail ride," she said. "They like to keep the groups small. But one of the people was a staff member named Jane, and she's running a talent show. I've signed up for it."

"Of course you have, dear! When is it?"

"Saturday night," Lisa said. "The night before we leave."

"Now, that's something to look forward to," said her mother. "What are you doing?"

"I guess I'm just in the chorus," she said. "It's mostly just silly skits, but it's kind of fun to be a part of it."

"Aren't you going to do a solo?" her mother asked.

"It's vacation," Lisa said.

"Well, singing beautifully isn't exactly like work for you, dear."

"I don't know yet, Mom," Lisa said, realizing she was skating close to the subject of "the boy." So she changed the subject again. "I went snorkeling this afternoon, too," she said. "I thought it was really cool, even though the coral reef by the beach here at the resort is pretty small. But I was amazed at the different colors of the coral. Do you know why that is, Dad?"

"I think what you're talking about is actually different kinds of coral," he said. "While we think of it as a single thing—coral—it's actually many, many different species, and each is unique and identifiable. One of the qualities that varies among the species is color. . . ."

He was off and running. Asking her father a technical question was very much like asking Carole about insect pests and horses. "Oh, we just spray them," was never the answer. It didn't surprise Lisa at all that her father had spent some time in the resort library looking up coral while her mother had been getting ready for the trip into town. Lisa had completely and successfully deflected her mother's inevitable questions about Tec Morrison.

Those questions would come sooner or later, but later Lisa might be able to answer them better, and later was when she was going to have to work with her parents to find a way to get her to Tec's town or find a way for him to come to Willow Creek.

"Of course, part of what makes each species a specific color probably relates to what they eat—like the pink of a flamingo coming from their diet of shrimp, and you know chickens that are fed corn have yellow skin—"

"I never knew any of that stuff, Dad," Lisa said, interrupting the explanation.

"Well, it's amazing what you can learn with just a quick stop in a library," he said.

"What are you up to tonight?" Mrs. Atwood asked.

"I guess I'll hang out with those kids," she said, nodding at the now empty table. "I'm meeting them in the lounge, and there was talk about going dancing later."

"At the disco?" her father asked. "Your mother and I were talking about stopping by there later."

"Um, I don't know, Dad. You know, we're just hanging out."

"Maybe we'll see you there," said Mr. Atwood.

Lisa sincerely hoped that would not be the case.

"Later, then," she said, excusing herself from the table. It was nice to see her parents happy, but it would be even nicer to see Tec.

THE LOUNGE WAS totally filled by the time Lisa arrived. It took her a few minutes to spot Tec and the other kids. They'd commandeered a corner table and each had a glass of soda. Tec had his back to the door, so he did not see Lisa arriving.

Kiki looked over her shoulder and spotted Lisa. Lisa smiled and waved. Kiki just looked back at the circle of friends. Will saw her then and welcomed her, pulling a chair over next to Tec. Lisa took it gratefully. There were three other girls there who hadn't been at the dinner table and they were introduced as Shelley, Erin, and Jackie. Lisa had to look twice. She was pretty sure that Shelley was the skinny girl in the skimpy bikini that she'd seen at the swimming pool with the guy who looked like Tec that afternoon, but she wasn't certain.

"Were those your *parents* you had dinner with?" Kiki asked.

"Guilty as charged," Lisa said, uncertain why she felt it necessary to defend herself—or her parents. She suspected most of the kids there had parents at the resort as well. It seemed likely that they would have occasional meals with them, and it didn't seem necessary to make a big deal of it. Lisa shrugged off the question and settled into her chair.

"I'm getting myself something to drink, Lisa. Can I get you something, too?" Tec asked, standing up.

"Oh, sure, thanks," she said. "I'll have a pineapple punch."

"Coming up," he said and slid off to the bar.

"He is *sooooo* cute," Sophie whispered, eyeing Tec while he stood at the bar.

She'd said it to the group, but Lisa knew it was intended to be heard by the girls and especially by her, because she was the one lucky enough to be his girlfriend.

"Don't I know it!" Shelley said.

"So, what am I?" Will interjected. "Chopped liver?"

Sophie, Shelley, and the other girls laughed. Kiki, caustic as ever, answered Will, "No, I think you're more like unchopped liver." That made her laugh, but nobody else joined in.

Erin turned to Lisa then: "Were you in the beach volleyball game this morning?" she asked.

"Nope," said Lisa. "I was on the beach on the other side of that hill." She pointed to where the trail ride had taken her.

"What were you doing over there?" Erin asked. "I mean, is it something special?"

"Very special," Lisa told her. "I went with a—"

"Here you go," Tec said, putting the drink down in front of her and smiling that smile that melted her knees.

"Thanks so much," she said, smiling back at him. She was relieved that he'd returned. There were some weird vibes at the table, and she felt more comfortable having him there with her.

"Okay, so what were you guys laughing about while I was gone?" Tec asked.

"We were talking about this morning's beach volleyball game," Jackie told him. "I bet you our team will win tomorrow!"

"Oh, well, we'll just have to see about that!" Tec said.

As Lisa listened, she realized that the group had met at a beach volleyball game that morning while she'd been riding. That was okay. She'd rather ride horses than play beach volleyball any time, so although she wouldn't have minded meeting this crew of kids before tonight, she didn't think she'd missed much.

"How about some pool?" Grant asked.

"I don't feel like swimming," Alex said.

"No, pool, like on a table," said Grant.

"Great," said Alex. Lisa hadn't known there were pool tables at the resort, and pool was something she'd never tried before. It sounded like fun. A couple of people decided to go for a walk instead, but most of the group wanted to play.

As they stood up to go to the game room, Lisa wondered if Tec would take her hand. It wasn't easy to be near him and to want to feel him touch her. She was a little disappointed when he didn't. In fact, as the group walked to the game room, Tec was having a conversation with Shelley and Grant—apparently about the next day's volleyball match.

Lisa hadn't been to the game room before. She followed the others and was a little surprised to find that it was quite close to the stable. She'd walked past it twice that day and just hadn't noticed it.

"What is that smell?" Kiki asked, pinching her nose with a big show.

"What smell?" Brain asked.

"*That* smell," Kiki said. Not that that identified the

offensive odor, but it was obvious what she meant when she pointed toward the stable.

"I think you mean the smell of horses," said Grant.

"It's not a bad smell," said Erin.

"Not at all," said Lisa. She'd always liked the smell of a barn, with the warm scents of horses, fresh hay, and leather and saddle soap. The only time a stable smelled bad was when it wasn't kept clean. A soiled stall could stink up a barn in a very short time. Max would never let that happen at Pine Hollow, and Lisa was certain that Frank would never let that happen here. In fact, as she sniffed the cool evening air, she could only smell the sweetest of barn smells. "It's a very clean barn," she began, remembering that she'd wanted to remind Tec about taking a trail ride in the morning.

"Barns always smell," said Kiki. "I mean, they're full of horses, and that means they're full of you-know-what."

Lisa presumed she meant manure and opened her mouth to explain the difference between manure and other animals' droppings, the reason it made good fertilizer, and, in general, how the horse's digestive system worked. The fact that all the kids were laughing at what Kiki had said made her pause, though. Even Tec was laughing.

Lisa closed her mouth. She knew the smell of horses

and barns wasn't everybody's favorite smell, and she realized this wasn't a group that would appreciate a
Carole-style discussion of manure. Also, to tell the
truth, manure wasn't the nicest part about being around
horses; it was just a fact of life, and there was no need
for her to stand up for a fact of life, even if it was a
horse's life.

"It won't smell inside the game room," said Brian,
opening the door. They all filed in, and Lisa was relieved to find that he was right. There was no hint of
the barn inside.

"Okay, so who wants to play first?" Grant asked.

There were two pool tables and they decided to play
teams; that meant that eight people could play at a
time. Lisa had never held a pool stick and found herself
reluctant to start with this crowd—all of whom seemed
to know how to do everything. She let others play. That
left her and Shelley and two others out of the games.

"How about some Ping-Pong?" she asked Shelley.

"Sure," the slender girl agreed.

The Ping-Pong tables were on the other side of the
room from the pool tables. It seemed relatively quiet
there. Lisa picked up the paddles and the ball, then
handed a paddle to the other girl.

They began to volley for the right to serve first. Shelley lost immediately. It wasn't that Lisa was a champion

Ping-Pong player; it just appeared that Shelley had never had a Ping-Pong paddle in her hand before. It became clear almost immediately that playing a game wasn't going to have much point to it, so they idly paddled the ball back and forth.

"I guess I'm not much of an athlete," Shelley said lamely.

"I saw you in the pool earlier today. You seemed to do just fine there," she said.

"Well, that was just having fun—"

"So's this," said Lisa.

"You think so?" Shelley asked.

"Not if it's no fun for you," said Lisa. "Would you rather watch the pool games?"

"I guess," Shelley said, putting her paddle down at just the moment that Lisa delivered a gentle lob she'd thought Shelley could handle and return to her. Lisa chased the ball, returned it to the table, and followed Shelley back to the benches near the pool tables.

Lisa thought the whole Ping-Pong thing had been very strange. Why had Shelley said she'd like to play if she couldn't do it at all? Why had she stopped so suddenly? Some of these kids were a little weird, and Shelley apparently fell into that category.

Lisa tried to make conversation with her. She asked her where she came from. Colorado. No, she didn't ski.

She wasn't a mountain climber. Lisa asked her where she went to school. It turned out she was a sopho-more. She asked Lisa what class she was in. Lisa told her she'd be a freshman next year.

"Oh, you're going to find college so different from high school!" Shelley said.

Lisa realized Shelley was assuming that by Lisa's freshman year, she meant freshman year in college, not Willow Creek High School. Lisa was about to correct her when it occurred to her that a number of these kids might be in college. If she admitted that she wasn't even in high school yet, what were they going to think of her? She felt a little special being able to hang out with college students, and she didn't want to mess that up by admitting she was at least four years younger than they were.

That was odd. Mostly, people thought Lisa was younger than she actually was. She was a year older than Carole and Stevie, but nobody ever thought much about that. Maybe wearing casual clothes, bathing suits, shorts, and sundresses sort of equalized everybody. She decided she wasn't going to be the one to unequalize them. She wasn't going to lie, she just wasn't going to straighten anybody out, either.

Besides, Tec had told her he was a sophomore in high school. He probably hadn't told any of the college kids that he was younger, either. That realization drew Lisa even closer to Tec—if that was possible.

"We win! We win! Who wants to play now?" Grant asked, inviting Lisa and Shelley over to the pool tables.

"Sure," said Lisa. "Are Shelley and I playing against you two?" she asked, looking at Grant and Tec.

"No. Lisa, you partner up with Tec, and I'll get Shelley. I can't wait to show her how to use a pool cue."

Grant's idea of showing Shelley what to do mostly involved him putting his arms around her while she leaned over the table. Shelley didn't seem to mind at all. Lisa found it a little embarrassing and was relieved when Tec didn't do the same thing with her.

Grant was being so silly about Shelley that it was easy for Lisa and Tec to beat them, even though it was almost always Tec who made the shots.

Lisa was just beginning to get the hang of pool and was ready to try another game when Alex announced that there was a movie on at the video center and suggested they all go to that.

A few of the kids wanted to see it, but Lisa wasn't interested. It was a sci-fi horror movie and not really her thing. Tec didn't want to go, either. A couple of the kids decided to go; the others wanted to go back to the lounge.

"I'll see you at the disco, right?" Shelley asked generally.

"Sure," most of the kids said.

Lisa had read in the brochure that the disco opened at ten every night and played until the last patron left— or until dawn, whichever came first. In spite of her long nap, she didn't think she'd be able to stay up much longer, but she also had a feeling that Shelley didn't much care if she showed up or not. She just nodded amid a whole group of *yeahs*, and *see you there laters*.

The group, at one moment tightly assembled outside the game room, was suddenly totally dispersed except for Lisa and Tec.

"That was fun," Lisa said, meaning it. It seemed that doing something—anything—with Tec was fun, no matter how weird some of the others were.

"And I've got an idea of something more fun," he said. There was an inviting sparkle in his eye.

"And that is?" she asked, smiling up at him.

"A midnight swim."

Lisa glanced at her watch. "It's only ten-thirty," she said.

"It must be midnight somewhere," he said, smiling back at her—that knee-melting, dimpled smile.

"How right you are," she said. "I'll go get my suit and meet you at the snorkeling beach in, say, ten minutes?"

"Do you really need to get your suit?" he asked.

"I can't swim in this," she said, looking down at her cotton dress.

"I—Well," Tec stammered. When Lisa realized what Tec had said, she was blushing with embarrassment.

"I was just teasing," he said. "You're such a good swimmer, I assumed you always had a suit on under everything."

"Not exactly," Lisa said. "But I'll see you in ten."

"It's a deal."

Lisa hurried to her cabin and changed, arriving at the beach with a towel in less than the agreed ten minutes. Tec was waiting for her.

"Nice to swim without worrying about a sunburn," Lisa said.

He smiled at her, took her hand, and together they dived into the waves.

An hour later, Tec walked Lisa back to her room. He was holding her towel warmly around her shoulders to protect her from the evening breeze, but she knew she wouldn't have noticed it if they'd been walking on an iceberg. The two of them had really enjoyed their nighttime swim, splashing one another and playing in the gentle surf before sitting on the beach in the moonlight, where they'd talked and talked, as they had the night before.

At Lisa's fifth yawn, Tec had remarked that she must be bored.

"Not a bit of it," she said. "But I am a little tired. I stayed up late last night and then got up early this morning and there was nowhere near enough time for napping."

"There never is in a cool place like this," Tec said. "There's too much to do to waste any time on something so unimportant as sleep. . . ."

Lisa had yawned again. "Speak for yourself," she said.

"Then I've got to get you back to your room," Tec said. He stood up, brushed the sand off his bathing trunks, and gave Lisa a hand standing up.

Walking back toward her room, Lisa knew she'd sleep well that night and have sweet dreams to boot.

Tec kissed her good night and told her he'd see her in the sunlight. She practically floated into her room.

It wasn't until she'd gotten into her nightgown that she realized she'd forgotten to tell Tec about the trail ride and the talent show. There always seemed to be so much to talk about that she forget everything!

She slipped back into her dress, hurried across the compound to Tec's room, and knocked on the door, sure she'd find him getting ready for bed, too. But there was no answer. Lisa realized that he was almost certainly taking a shower to get the saltwater and sand off before he went to sleep. It wasn't yet midnight. He was bound to be at breakfast in time for her to tell him about the trail ride, and then she could tell him about the show while they were riding.

Lisa left the darkened door and returned to her own room and her own dreams.

"Lorraine, you missed a spot," Stevie said.

Lorraine, perched atop a ladder, looked where she'd just been painting and reached for the area again with her paintbrush.

"No, farther to the left," Stevie said.

"Here?" Lorraine asked.

"Yes, that's it," said Stevie, satisfied. She turned her attention elsewhere. "Meg, don't forget to use up and down strokes. That way we'll avoid blotches and smears."

"Yes, Stevie," Meg responded obediently, switching from her prior cross-pattern stroking.

"Joe, have you found the extender for the ceiling roller?" Stevie asked without even turning around.

"I've got it and I've got it working," he said. Stevie looked over her shoulder to where Joe was standing with the long-handled roller, painting the ceiling a nice gleaming white—the same color as the rest of the room.

Carole watched her friend in action, almost astonished at what she was seeing. What didn't astonish her was how easily Stevie was taking to the job of boss of the project. There might be some people who would criticize Stevie as being *bossy* of the project, but everyone in the room at that moment would have agreed that whatever Stevie was doing, it was working. Under her firm hand and eagle eye, the tack room was being totally transformed from a dusty, soiled mess, covered with peeling paint, to a gleaming white, clean space. They were all proud of the job that was getting done, but no one was prouder than Stevie.

"Good job, crew! Good job. In fact, I think you're doing a better job than yesterday's early evening crew."

"I was on that crew," Joe Novick said. "And you said the same thing about us compared to the afternoon crew."

"I was right then and I'm right now," Stevie announced.

"And what about this afternoon's crew?" Meg teased.

"They'll be better than you are—especially if you don't stop talking and stay focused on your job."

Carole, resting from her stint with a paintbrush, looked over the chart that she and Stevie had devised at the beginning of the project. The first piece of really good news was that absolutely everybody had showed up when they'd said they would, except for Adam Levine, who'd developed a case of the flu and had his doctor write a note for Stevie. The other piece of good news was that not only were they on schedule, they were ahead of schedule. The first coat would be finished that day, and the second coat couldn't possibly take more than another day. Then all that would be left to do would be to move all the tack back into the room when the paint was dry. It was amazing what could be done when a group of dedicated workers hung together to get a worthwhile project finished!

"Stevie! Are you in there?" It was Mrs. Reg.

"Right here," Stevie volunteered. Not that Mrs. Reg had really paused for an answer.

"Well, that's good becau—Oh my!" she said, stopping dead in her tracks.

"What's the matter?" Carole asked. Mrs. Reg was rarely speechless, and at that moment, she clearly couldn't say anything.

"I—I, uh. Oh my!" She repeated herself.

Carole was more than a little curious about what had silenced her. "Good or bad?" she asked.

Mrs. Reg nodded.

"Good?"

She nodded again.

"Get the lady a chair, Betsy!" Stevie said.

Betsy Cavanaugh pulled a small bench out of the hallway and offered it to Mrs. Reg, who sat down, still holding her right hand against her heart.

"Oh my!"

"What's up, Mrs. Reg?" Stevie asked, undaunted by Mrs. Reg's condition.

"You're really doing it!" she said. "You're going to finish on time, and it's going to look wonderful!"

"You doubted us?" Stevie asked.

Mrs. Reg's jaw closed then. She swallowed. "I think you doubted yourselves," she reminded Stevie.

"Oh, right. I remember that," Stevie said. "That was back when we'd bitten off more than we could chew."

"Just like it was two days ago," Mrs. Reg said, regaining her composure.

"That, too," Stevie agreed. "Anyway, what's up?"

"Oh, right. You have a phone call," Mrs. Reg told her. "If you want, you can take it in my office."

"Sure," Stevie said. She got down off her stool and handed Mrs. Reg her clipboard. "Why don't you take over for a few minutes while I get the phone."

Mrs. Reg nodded, still more than a little surprised, accepting Stevie's clipboard with the full schedule on it. Carole knew that a mere glance would confirm to her that the job was going to be done very soon. Mrs. Reg grinned.

Stevie hurried down the stable's aisle and saw the phone lying on Mrs. Reg's desk. It wasn't until then that it really occurred to her to wonder who would be calling her at the stable on a Tuesday morning.

"Hello?" she said.

"Hi, Stevie, it's Phil."

"Hi, Phil, what's up?" Stevie asked.

"Listen, I just called because I feel bad about what happened—me saying I'd help and then finking. I know it's a little late to get started on a big project like that, but A.J. and I will be back tomorrow afternoon—"

"I thought you were skiing," Stevie said.

"We would be, if we'd brought wet suits," said Phil.

"Wet suits?"

"It's about fifty degrees up here and it's pouring rain. It's been raining since we arrived and there's no end in sight. In weather like this, they can't even make artificial snow. We've spent the entire time playing video games—something we could have been doing at home, if we hadn't intended to come help you paint."

115

"Listen, Phil, I'm pretty busy right now," Stevie said.

"I guess," said Phil.

"I'm sorry the skiing hasn't worked out—"

"You are?"

"Why wouldn't I be?" Stevie asked. "Anyway, call me when you get home, okay? If I'm not at my house, I'll be here."

"Stevie, I'm really sorry. I mean it. I—I didn't do the right thing," he stammered.

"It's okay, Phil. I'll talk to you when you get back. Right?"

"Right," he said. "And if you want to feed me some crow—"

"Bye," Stevie said. She hung up the phone.

How strange, she thought. *Two days ago, I would have jumped around gleefully to learn that Phil was having a miserable time. Now, I even feel a little sorry for him!*

She knew Carole would be amused to hear about Phil's busted skiing trip. She wished Lisa were there to hear about it as well.

"YOU'RE RIDING MUCH better this morning," Frank said.

Lisa wasn't surprised. She was riding a better horse and she was better prepared. She'd also had a better night's sleep. In fact, the only thing that was missing was Tec. She'd hoped he would remember about the trail ride and get there that morning, but there had been no sign of him at breakfast or around the pool or beaches. She wasn't going to miss a trail ride on account of him, though. No matter how Tec melted her knees with his grin and made her feel wonderful when he kissed her, it didn't change the way she felt about horses.

Once again, Jane was there. Lisa wasn't sure if Jane was riding for pleasure or if it was part of her job to be assistant trail boss. It didn't much matter. Lisa liked her and was glad to talk with her.

Jane told her about some of the people who were planning to audition for solos that day.

"I think your list is going to get longer," Lisa said.

"How's that?" Jane asked while they trotted on a path that wound between palm trees.

"Remember that guy I told you about?"

"The one who didn't make it to rehearsal?"

"Right, well, he's a real performer, too. He's playing Artful Dodger in *Oliver!* at his school this spring."

"High-school production?" Jane asked.

Lisa nodded. "He's really good, I'm sure," she said.

"Maybe," Jane asked. "But I won't know until he auditions."

"Well, I'm going to get him to do some kind of duet with me—like 'Anything You Can Do.' Wouldn't that be neat?"

"Why don't you just do a solo?" Jane asked.

Lisa wondered why she was being so skeptical about Tec, but she knew the reality was a lot of kids who were good enough to perform in their high schools weren't good enough to perform with a group of adults. That had to be the reason.

"I could, I guess," Lisa said. "I still remember 'Tomorrow.' "

"And we've got a cute red dress that would do nicely for the part," Jane said.

"But I haven't auditioned yet," said Lisa.

"You'll still have to," Jane told her. "But I've heard you sing, and I've watched you on stage. You know what you're doing, and you'll do fine."

"Tec knows what he's doing, too."

"Tec didn't come to the rehearsal," Jane reminded her.

"But he'll come to the audition today and the rehearsal, and you'll see what I mean," Lisa said.

"Maybe," said Jane. "But if he's not there today, then I think we'll have to go without him. I know this is just a silly talent show for an audience made up of friends and family members, but I need to have the cast prepared and committed."

At that moment, Frank signaled all the riders to change to a canter. Lisa nudged her horse into the faster gait.

Jane was being a little tough, but she was right. If there were only going to be a couple of rehearsals, it would make a big difference if someone missed them. There was only so much that Lisa would be able to explain to Tec. He'd have to come to the audition and to the rest of the rehearsals. Lisa was pretty sure he would, and she was looking forward to showing Jane that she'd known what she was talking about.

This day's ride was along a different and more difficult path than the ride the previous morning. It took a lot of concentration because it was unfamiliar terrain. One thing Lisa had learned from other experiences riding on beaches was that a horse moved very differently depending on how solid the sand was under its hooves. Wet sand responded like firm earth. Soft, dry sand seemed to suck the hooves into its warmth and slowed the horse's gait considerably. If she didn't pay attention to where she was going, she might end up going nowhere fast.

She focused on the pleasurable task in front of her and pushed all thoughts of the talent show out of her mind until the group returned to the barn.

"I hope you don't think I'm an old meany," Jane said, loosening her horse's girth.

"Not at all," Lisa said. "You're right and I know it. But I think I'm right, too. Wait until you see what he can do."

"I'll be only too happy to welcome this guy to the cast," said Jane. "I mean that."

"And you will," Lisa said, handing her reins over to a stable hand. "See you later."

"Definitely," Jane said.

Lisa walked back to her cabin, noticing the game room as she passed by and wondering what Kiki would think of the way she smelled right then. It made her laugh, and then it made her think of Tec. It was a little odd that he would hang around with someone like Kiki—especially when he could have spent more time with Lisa instead!

That thought made Lisa wonder when she'd see him again, and before she did, she intended to wash the scent of horse sweat completely off.

Lisa had finished her shower and was putting on her bathing suit and cover-up when there was a knock at her door.

She peered outside hopefully.

"Hi, sweetie." It was her father.

"Hi, Dad."

"Your mom and I are going to play a round of golf at a nearby club and have lunch over there. Would you like to come along? You could . . . well, drive the cart if you'd like."

Drive the cart? With her parents? Was he nuts? No,

Lisa realized. It was his way of saying they'd be away and they cared about her.

"Um, no thanks, Dad. I think I'll hang out here," she said. "I'll see you at dinner, okay?"

"Okay, Lisa," he said. He kissed her forehead.

Ten minutes later, Lisa was making her way along the beach, hoping for a glimpse of—there he was. Tec was lounging on a beach chair in the middle of a large group of kids, most of whom he and Lisa had been with the night before, and some others as well.

Tec smiled at Lisa. "Hey, where have you been this morning?" he asked.

"I was riding," she said.

"Horses?" he asked.

"Yes, remember I mentioned the trail ride? I thought you might like to come . . . ?"

"You'd never get Tec to wear one of those dorky hats," Kiki said, intruding on their conversation.

That was fairly typical of Kiki—she always had a cutting remark at hand. It occurred to Lisa that Kiki would do well to have a Carole-like explanation of the very real safety concerns that were addressed with a solid riding helmet, but before she could take the first deep breath to begin the talk, others began talking about riding helmets and Tec.

"Sure," Shelley said. "Like Tec would ever risk having

his hair mussed with one of those things. He'd get helmet hair!" She laughed hysterically. Kiki joined in, as did a number of the other kids. Lisa saw no way out. She laughed, too.

Besides, they were right. A riding helmet really did a number on her hair every time she wore one.

The best part was that Tec was laughing, too; and when he laughed, he smiled; and when he smiled, his dimples blossomed; and when that happened, Lisa's knees melted and everything was right with the universe.

Tec patted the empty chair next to him. "Come sit down next to me," he invited her. Lisa was only too happy to comply.

11

"CHECK THIS OUT, Stevie!" Carole called to her friend. Stevie stepped out of the tack room and took a deep breath. She'd been in the stuffy, fume-filled room for so long that she'd forgotten what fresh air smelled like! That wasn't what Carole was calling about, however.

Stevie followed her friend's voice to what was known at Pine Hollow as the hat wall. It was outside the locker area—a large wall containing rows and rows of long nails that held the stable's riding hats. Most riders who rode owned their own hats. Those who didn't could always find something (often abandoned or outgrown hats) on the hat wall. Over the years, the hat wall itself had become less than sparkling white. Today, however, it gleamed with two coats of fresh paint.

"Why didn't I think of that?" Stevie asked, admiring Polly and April's work.

"Because you were busy doing something more important," April said. "And besides, Polly and I weren't on the schedule for this afternoon, and there wasn't room for us in the tack room. That's when we spotted this little mess and decided to take matters into our own hands."

"Good job!" Stevie declared. "Max is going to be blown away when he sees what we've accomplished while he's been gone."

"It may make him want to go away again," Carole remarked.

"No, next time, we get to go away, and he and Deborah can stay home and paint," Stevie said.

"We're out of paint in here!" Joe called from the tack room.

"I'll get it," Carole said, knowing that Stevie could use another minute away from the fumes.

Stevie stood back and admired the clean wall where the hats hung. "I think it needs something special," she said.

It had sometimes been Stevie's habit to use the hat wall as a sort of message board, hanging hats on the nails so that they spelled something. It only took Stevie a few seconds to come to an obvious conclusion. The fast-drying paint was already completely dry. She sorted the hats on the floor in front of her by size and then began hanging them up in their new order. April and Polly stood back and watched.

It didn't take long. Stevie had them hung up to spell MAX!

"Cute," said April. "He's going to love it."

"He will, Stevie," said a new voice. It was Mrs. Reg. Stevie wasn't accustomed to getting much in the way of compliments from Mrs. Reg, and it felt really good to get two from her in one day.

"Think so?" Stevie asked.

"I know so," said Mrs. Reg, patting Stevie on the shoulder. "You've been working so hard on this project that I may just let you off the hook for tack polishing for a long time to come!"

"You mean, like months?" Stevie asked. It was unlike Mrs. Reg to let any opportunity pass to put a rider to work on something—especially tack cleaning.

"No, I mean like two or three days!" she teased.

"Whatever," Stevie said, sweeping her hair off her forehead with a paint-splattered wrist, leaving a long white smear as she went.

Stevie and Mrs. Reg were still admiring the freshly painted hat wall when Veronica sauntered past.

"What's that?" she asked, brushing some plaster dust off her otherwise immaculate riding pants.

"The result of something known as w-o-r-k," said Stevie.

Veronica didn't respond to the snide remark. Instead, she just walked up to the hat wall and began moving the helmets around. In a few seconds, she'd transformed the M into a *T* and the exclamation point into an *I*. "Taxi!" she called out, as if she were flagging one for herself— and just to make sure everyone noticed the clever transformation she'd managed.

"I'd be glad to call you a taxi," Stevie said. "To take you home!"

"Hey! You're a taxi!" said April, giggling at her own joke.

Veronica walked on, still brushing at the long-gone plaster dust.

Stevie shifted the hats back to MAX!, not minding that Veronica was being a pain. Even Veronica couldn't spoil a day like this.

She went back into the tack room to find Carole. It was time to begin thinking about what kind of celebration they'd have.

JANE HAD BEEN right. Tec wasn't going to be in the show and Lisa had no intention of begging him. He'd already made a plan for the afternoon to go on a cruise in the resort's boat. A lot of the other kids were going, too. She knew she'd have fun if she went with them, but she was committed to the talent show, and that afternoon she was going to do her audition. In a way, it almost made it better. That meant Tec would be in the audience. She was good onstage, and now Tec would see it from the best possible perspective. She'd sing "Tomorrow," and he'd know it was for him.

"I would have told you about the cruise so you could have come along," he had said while they were at the buffet, getting desserts.

"It's okay, really. I don't mind. I've got something I want to do this afternoon, so even if you could get me a reservation now, I wouldn't be able to go. But it sounds like fun."

"Sure," he said. "But it would be more fun if you were going to be there." He reached out and patted her cheek, which was, by then, totally red with a blush.

"Well, I'll see you at dinner," she said.

"It's a deal," he told her. "Bye for now."

He tucked an apple and two cookies into his shirt pockets and left the dining room, followed by most of the group of kids they'd been with at the beach that morning. Shelley linked her arm through Tec's on one side and Brian's on the other as they walked out.

Yech, Lisa said to herself. She was having a lot of trouble warming to Shelley.

Lisa rejoined the few kids who weren't going on the cruise and finished her dessert without saying much to them. Their conversation revolved around things that had happened at the disco the night before when Lisa had been sound asleep. It had nothing to do with her. When she'd finished her fruit salad, she excused herself and headed for the theater.

Jane was there, working on some of the blocking and waiting for auditioners.

"No singing partner?" Jane asked.

"Off on a cruise for the afternoon," Lisa said.

"I'm sorry," Jane said.

"I'm not," Lisa told her. "You were right. He's got a lot going on, and I guess he's going to be too busy for rehearsals anyway. It's just me."

"And that's fine, too," Jane said. "Now, sing for me."

It took Jane a few minutes to find the right sheet music, but once she had she sat down at the piano and struck the series of chords that were totally and wonderfully familiar to Lisa. She began, "The sun'll come out tomorrow. . . ."

Jane played all the way through the song, and Lisa was delighted to sing all the verses, which she still remembered perfectly. She'd never performed it without other people onstage, but she took to the solo role just fine, judging by the grin on Jane's face.

"You're great!" Jane said after she'd finished playing the last notes. "I don't know why you thought you needed a singing partner for anything at all. The audience is going to love you!"

Lisa was pleased, and she had no intention of telling Jane that she didn't care a whit what most people in the audience thought of her. There was only one person there whom she wanted to have love her, tomorrow and always.

"I've got several other people to hear now, and then we're going to work on costumes. Like I said, I think we've got something that'll pass for Annie's dress. In the meantime, you can help Eddie sort out the fairy costumes. . . ."

Lisa helped Eddie sort out the costumes. She also helped him iron the frog's outfit and sew up the split seam on the back half of the cow. After that, she and Eddie and Ramon put sparkly paint on the undersea flats and hammered in some loose nails on the barnyard fence.

In the background, she could hear other people auditioning for solos. There was a woman who was under the severe misimpression that she could carry a tune—so severe that she'd brought her own sheet music and costume with her. Jane had to explain to her as nicely as possible that the show was already too long and, well . . .

It turned out there was a juggler in their midst. A man from Idaho had a wonderful act in which he juggled a conch shell, a chunk of coral, and a beanbag. He was very funny, sitting on a stool pretending he was on a unicycle. Jane explained to him that the show was *not* too long at all and they'd be more than happy to have him join the cast.

A couple of other singers and a piano player auditioned as well, and Jane conceded that the show had room for one more singer and one more piano player. Lisa was impressed with the way Jane handled the talented and the untalented. She was pleased to be among the former and was happy to tell the juggler how funny he was when he joined the crew and began juggling stuffed chickens from the barnyard set.

"Okay, costume time," Jane said.

The juggler didn't need anything, and the other singer was just going to wear her own dress, so that wasn't a problem. The piano player said he'd do just fine in shorts and a T-shirt, so the only person who needed a costume was Lisa.

"I can just wear my own dress," she told Jane.

"Like I said, I think there's something very Annie-like in here."

Lisa followed her into the costume room. It reminded her of nothing so much as the tack room at Pine Hollow. Gowns, pants, shirts, skirts, and crazy hats seemed to flow out of the wall, and she strongly suspected there was as tight an organizational plan in effect here as there was at Pine Hollow.

Jane walked right to the dress she wanted. "Here we go," she said, pulling a hanger off a rack. The dress was, in fact, Annie's very red dress, a mere two sizes too big for Lisa.

"Eddie! Ramon! Get in here!" she called out.

Eddie and Ramon arrived.

"Not a problem," Ramon declared.

"Follow me," said Eddie.

Lisa did.

Fifteen minutes later, she was back out in the sunshine, having been told to relax until the official rehearsal began.

It wasn't easy resting when so much was going on in her mind. In one corner, she was wondering how the cruise was going, hoping that Tec was having fun (but not too much fun), and sort of hoping that Shelley wasn't having any fun at all and that Kiki had fallen overboard. In another corner, she was running over the steps in the dances she was doing and making sure she remembered all the words to all the songs (she did). In most of her mind, though, she was thinking about how much Tec was going to love it when she sang to him—

not that anyone else in the audience was going to know that that was what she was doing.

An hour later she was too busy to think. The rehearsal was extremely intense and extremely tiring. A lot of the participants had forgotten words, cues, and dance steps. Lisa seemed to have a better memory than most and helped out.

Then the time came for her to sing her solo for the performers.

They loved it. They clapped and stomped for her and patted her on the back and told her she was great.

Lisa grinned, feeling even better inside than out, because she knew it was going to be great.

Then Eddie and Ramon came out from backstage and gave her exactly what she needed—a completely resized Annie dress.

"Perfect!" she declared.

Tec was going to love it!

"THAT'S IT, STEVIE," Adam reported, flashing a small salute. "The last bridle is back in its place!"

"I can't believe it," Stevie said. "Done, and we still have a couple of days to go before Max gets back. You guys are something!"

"We couldn't have done it without, um—" Betsy began and then paused.

"Our boss," April supplied. Stevie suspected that was nicer than what Betsy had been going to say, but she knew that everybody was proud of the job they'd done, and even if she'd been a little bossy from time to time, it had worked.

There was a general cheer before the helpers began

picking up the paintbrushes and putting the equipment away.

"I'm going to give the feed room a final check," Carole said. "It would be really easy to leave a bridle or a box of bits or a bunch of stirrup irons in there."

"I'll come check, too," Stevie said, following her friend down the hall.

What they saw in the feed room really surprised them. It was the feed room all right, and it didn't look one tiny bit different than it had four days ago, before the whole project had begun. And that was the problem.

It was a mess. The paint was old, dusty, and peeling. The ceiling was dark with a generation of dirt.

The girls didn't say anything. Stevie just glanced at her watch, and they returned to the bright and clean tack room.

"We think you'd better come see this," Carole said to the remains of their afternoon work crew.

The crew followed Carole and Stevie back to the feed room. Nobody said anything, because everybody saw the obvious.

"I don't want to do the ceiling again!" Joe wailed.

"I guess it's my turn for the really ugly tall-person job," said Adam, now recovered from the flu.

"You've got a deal," said Joe.

Without further ado, the crew began to move the feed bins to the center of the room. This job was going to go much faster, partly because it was a smaller room, but mostly because they didn't have to take everything out of it. All they needed to do was to shove everything in the center and put a drop cloth over it.

Stevie and Carole knew they'd be ready to begin serious painting by the time the late-afternoon crew showed up. One coat tonight, one tomorrow . . .

"OH, YOU SHOULD have seen your father trying to get out of that sand trap! We might just as well have stayed at the beach for all the time he spent digging in the sand!" Mrs. Atwood teased. Lisa's father was smiling at the ribbing.

The three of them were sitting together over dinner. There had been no sign of Tec, but the smiles on Lisa's parents' faces had been very inviting, and she was glad to be with them when they were in such good moods.

"I was really awful!" Mr. Atwood told Lisa. "On the other hand, your mother gave me some lessons in three-putting."

"And one in four-putting!" her mother said.

Lisa didn't know much about golf, but she knew that her parents had obviously had a good time playing, even though apparently they hadn't played very well.

"So who won?" Lisa asked.

"We both did," her father said. "I can't remember when I've had that much fun!"

"Me either," said Mrs. Atwood. "And what did you do?" she asked.

"I was here," Lisa said. "Actually, I spent most of the afternoon in the theater, working on the talent show. It's going to be great."

"Of course it is," said her mother. "You're going to be in it."

"Mom," Lisa protested.

"Your mother has a point," said her dad.

"You're just saying that because you're my parents," Lisa joked.

"We take our job seriously, as you can tell," her mother said. "And besides, you are talented and you always make us proud when you're onstage."

"Thanks. I hope this won't be an exception. I'll probably do okay, but the highlight is the juggler, believe me!"

"I'll be surprised if we like his performance better than yours," said her father. "But this is a week with a lot of highlights."

"I agree," said Lisa's mother, beaming.

"Me too," said Lisa.

"Family vacations are a good idea," said Mrs. Atwood.

"This one certainly is," said Mr. Atwood.

After dinner, her parents were going to play bridge with a couple they'd met at the golf club. They told Lisa she was welcome to sit in. Lisa couldn't imagine that that would be any fun at all—especially if she could find Tec anywhere.

"No thanks," she said. "I'll see you around, though." She excused herself and headed for the lounge, where she expected to find what she was beginning to think of as The Group.

There was no sign of them. Lisa was pretty sure they'd all be finished with dinner, so she kept on walking, wondering where to look. Perhaps the game room, though she wasn't much looking forward to another game of Ping-Pong. Fortunately they weren't there, and Lisa didn't have to go much farther to find them.

They were on the volleyball court, which was lit for night play.

"Hey, Lis! How's it going? Want to play?" Tec invited her as soon as he spotted her.

"Sure," she said.

"Come play on our side," Brian said. "We need all the help we can get!"

"Okay," she said, a little disappointed to be playing against Tec rather than with him, but it didn't matter. Volleyball was a fun game and a sport that she was good at. This would be fun no matter which side she played on.

Fortunately she was wearing sneakers and shorts, so she didn't have to change to join the game. She stood at the spot Brian indicated and waited for the serve.

It was a lively game. The ball swooped back and forth over the net and the teams were fairly well matched—until Shelley rotated into the front row of Lisa's team. She was wearing the skimpiest of string bikinis. In fact, it was the same one Lisa had seen her wearing the first time she'd seen her in the swimming pool. It might have been proper wear for a swim, but it hardly seemed adequate for a volleyball game. Shelley jumped and twisted, bumping and spiking. She was actually quite a good athlete, but Lisa was dead sure that that was the last thing that any of the boys on the other team—or even on her own team—were thinking about as her lithe, skinny body did those amazing things to the volleyball.

"Fifteen to four!" Brian declared. They'd won handily. Lisa was glad her team had won, but considering their secret weapon, she wasn't convinced any boy on the other team even noticed.

They played another game with approximately the same result. By then it was nine-thirty, and some of the kids—including Shelley—were talking about changing their clothes before going to the disco. The group dispersed with vague promises of *see you laters*, leaving Lisa and Tec and the volleyball, which had to be returned to the game room. They walked there together.

"How was the cruise?" she asked.

"Uh, oh, right. It was okay," he said.

"Were most of the kids there?"

"A lot of that crowd. I don't remember who, exactly. I missed you."

"Well, I missed you, too," said Lisa, smiling at him.

"What was it you were doing?" he asked. Lisa wondered why he didn't remember, but decided to take advantage of it with a surprise when the talent show came along. "You'll see, all in good time," she said. "On Saturday," she added.

"A surprise?"

"I think so," she said. She handed the volleyball to the clerk in the game room and the two of them turned toward the ocean. Tec took her hand and they began another wonderful walk in the starry moonlit night.

"It's hard to imagine this is all almost over," said Lisa. "It's going so fast!"

"Sure is," said Tec. "And even though I'm staying longer, it still seems like it's flying by."

"That's the way it is when you're having fun," said Lisa.

"Definitely," Tec agreed, squeezing her hand.

Lisa slipped out of her sneakers and began sloshing in the gentle waves that lapped at the shore. Tec joined her, taking her hand again.

"One of the things I haven't had a chance to do is teach you how to ride," Lisa said.

"Oh, right," said Tec.

"There'll be time when we get back to Virginia, though," she said.

He looked at her curiously. "We may be in the same state, but we live pretty far apart," he said.

"We'll find a way," she said, certain that somehow their love for one another would surpass the miles.

"My best friend's boyfriend lives far away, too," she told him. "And he comes over to our stable to ride all the time."

"Really?" said Tec. "Horses?"

"Sure, that's what we ride at Pine Hollow. You're going to love the place. The owner is a guy named Max and he's the greatest instructor. I mean, I can give you an idea of what you should be doing, but Max'll have you in top form in no time. There are a lot of great horses there. You'll probably start on Patch. Everybody does. But when you get a little better, Max might let you ride Topside. He's a Thoroughbred, like the horse I usually ride, Prancer. Both of them belong to the stable."

Lisa could have gone on, but something told her that

Tec wasn't really paying attention to what she was saying. Was it possible he'd just said he wanted to learn to ride horses because he thought she'd like him to say that—that he'd never love horses the way she did? Maybe. It didn't matter, though. There were a lot of couples who enjoyed doing different things and then had things they liked doing together. Like her parents, for example. They had a good time playing golf and bridge together. Her father couldn't stand shopping, and her mother hated it when he had business to do, even though he loved the work he did. She and Tec might be like that.

When she stopped talking, he looked at her. "You seem tired," he said.

"I am," she told him. "I've had a very long day, but I'm glad to be here with you now."

"And I'm glad you're here, too, but it's almost eleven now, and if you don't get some rest, you'll resent me in the morning."

"Never," she said.

"Tomorrow," he said. She wondered if he had any idea that he'd just said the very word she'd be singing to him in such a short time. She didn't ask. Nor did she have time to. He took her chin in his hand and tilted it up so that it was at the perfect angle for a perfect kiss.

Lisa's head was still full of moonlight, stars, and warm

tropical breezes when the door to her room closed behind her. This time, however, it only took her about four seconds to realize she'd forgotten to ask Tec about riding in the morning.

She opened the door and looked in the direction of his cabin. He wasn't there. She looked around the corner. He was heading back in the direction of the lounge.

"Tec!" she called. He stopped and turned around, walking back toward her.

"What's up?" he asked.

"I forgot to remind you that there's a trail ride in the morning. Would you like to come along?"

"I don't think so," he said. "I guess riding isn't for me."

"That's all right," she said. "I just wanted you to know you'd be welcome."

"Thanks, but I'll see you later then, okay?"

"Okay—and, um, good night."

She went back to her room, ready for a good night's sleep.

13

"WE'RE WONDERFUL. FABULOUS. Miraculous. Unbelievable," Stevie announced.

"Does that mean we're finished?" Meg Durham asked.

"Finally, completely, and totally," Stevie said.

She stood and looked at the feed room. The last bin was back where it belonged, the final bale of hay was back in the stack against the freshly painted wall.

"Are you sure you don't want us to paint the ladies' room?" Betsy asked.

"Does it need it?" Stevie asked in response.

"No!" Adam and Joe declared in a single voice. "At least, I don't think so," said Adam.

"It's tiled," April informed them. "No paint anywhere."

"Whew!"

Mrs. Reg appeared with a large tray of cookies and apple cider. "This is the very least I could do for this remarkable crew. Thank you one and all, and especially, thank you, Stevie."

"You're more than welcome, Mrs. Reg, but I've got to tell you it never could have been done without everybody pitching in. Just a couple of days ago, Carole and I thought we were sunk. Today, well, we're standing here in the middle of this freshly painted feed room, just feet away from a tack room that's the envy of every stable in the state of Virginia, and we couldn't have finished it in time without you. In fact, I'm not sure we could have done it at all. You all pitched in in a way that—well, it shows what teamwork can do. I can't thank you enough."

"It's okay, Stevie. You don't have to say anything else," Meg said. "Actually, I think we've all had enough speeches from you over the last few days!"

Everybody laughed, but everybody also knew that she meant that in the nicest possible way. Stevie had been a boss, but she'd also been the chief cheerleader and organizer. They held up their glasses of cider in a toast to her as she thanked each of them.

Red O'Malley appeared in the feed room and told Stevie she had a phone call.

She excused herself, wondering who would be calling her there.

It was Phil again.

"We're back. I thought we'd be back a couple of days ago, but we couldn't get a flight until this morning. Anyway, I've talked my mother into driving me over to Willow Creek this afternoon. I'll be there by two, and A.J. is coming, too. We're both wearing our painting clothes and we'll do anything—even the windows."

"You don't have to, Phil," Stevie began.

"No, I was really a fink," he said. "I made you a promise and then I broke it. I've been thinking about you and Carole slaving over those buckets of paint, and I felt just awful."

"So bad you couldn't ski?" she asked. She couldn't help herself.

"The rain saw to that," he said. "The whole vacation was a bust. We'd have done much better staying here and working with you. But I promise you, we're there for you now—or we will be. I mean, I know it isn't much at this point, what with Max getting back tomorrow, but maybe we can get a wall or two done. It'll be a start."

"You don't have to come," Stevie said.

"I know I don't *have* to. I *want* to," he told her.

"Don't worry about it," Stevie said. "Really."

"I'm not worried. And we'll both stay as long as you want."

"No, I mean you don't have to," Stevie said. "Some other people helped."

"Well, we can help, too," he said.

"There isn't anything to do," she told him.

"We really want to help," Phil said insistently. "What I did wasn't fair to you."

"Thanks, Phil, but it's just a tiny bit possible that I wasn't exactly fair to you, either."

"You weren't?"

"Not totally," she said. "See, what I hadn't realized was that it might be possible to get a couple of other people to pitch in over here."

"How many people have been helping you?" he asked.

Stevie glanced at her clipboard and the schedule that she still held in her hand. It took her a moment to count. "A dozen," she said finally. "We usually had four working here at a time, plus Carole and me, so that makes six, in three shifts each day—sometimes people stayed for double shifts—so that was a dozen workers. Oh, and it would have gone faster if it weren't for Dr. Faisal."

"Dr. Who?"

"The orthodontist," Stevie explained.

"What?"

"It's complicated, Phil."

"It always is with you, Stevie." He began to laugh a little.

"Anyway, I'm pretty sure I overreacted when I was so angry with you."

"I'm sorry, too," he said. Those were the words she'd been waiting to hear.

"It's okay, Phil. And it's worked out okay, too. Wait'll you see the place. We even painted the feed room!"

"I think I'd like to see it," said Phil.

"Why don't you come over next weekend and have a ride with us?"

"I'll be there—and I can't wait," he said.

"Me either," she answered truthfully.

IF LISA THOUGHT the first part of her vacation had gone quickly, she was totally unprepared for how fast the rest of it went. The days were a whirl of volleyball, swims, delicious meals, rehearsals, and morning trail rides. She'd even seen her parents a couple of times—and each time they'd been as cheerful as the last. This vacation had definitely been good for the whole Atwood family.

She'd spent more time with Tec, too, though not as much as she would have liked, and, she suspected, not as much as he would have liked, either. With her morning trail rides and her afternoon rehearsals, she'd missed a couple of trips he'd taken with the other kids. But that had still left time for moonlight walks and swims, one more snorkeling picnic by themselves, and lots of time with the other kids. Lisa wasn't finding that she liked most of them much better than she had at first, but she was getting used to them and they were getting used to her. She knew she'd never see most of them ever again, and that was fine, too.

And now it was Saturday—her last day on San Felipe. Tonight was the performance. Since she had to be at the theater early, she'd left Tec at the beach to get ready and eat an early dinner. She hadn't told him what she was up to, but she did tell him that she was about ready for his surprise and he should meet her at the talent show that night. *That ought to entice him*, she thought.

Lisa got to the dining room early enough that most of the other occupants were families with young children, and she didn't know any of them. It didn't matter that she didn't have friends to eat with; she wasn't very hungry and wasn't going to eat very much in any event. If she'd learned one thing about performing, it was that she shouldn't do it on a full stomach. Nerves could cause butterflies, and butterflies could cause indigestion. That was the last thing she'd need tonight!

She ate a banana and some toast and made her excuses to the other people at the table, who had barely noticed her presence anyway. She knew there would be a cast party after the show, and there would be plenty to eat and drink there—and it would be more fun eating with Tec, who could join her there, than with anyone else.

As she walked toward the theater she spotted him in the lounge, where he was getting himself a soda at the bar. She slipped in and greeted him.

"There you are!" he said. "Come join us."

"No, I've got to get going," she told him. "Remember, I've got a surprise for you tonight."

"How could I forget a promise like that?" he asked, smiling that smile that melted her knees.

"I'll see you at the show, okay?"

"Definitely," he told her. "I'm looking forward to it." And then his lips brushed her cheek before he returned to the circle where the other kids were waiting for him. For a moment, Lisa wondered how it was that she'd made it through all the years she'd lived so far without Tec Morrison.

She waved at the others, wondering briefly what they'd think of her performance, and headed to the theater.

They'd been called to get there at six-thirty for a final run-through. Some of the skits were still rougher than

Lisa thought they ought to be, but she knew this was just for fun, and if some of the chorus members flubbed some acts, well, it didn't matter. She also knew that she was determined not to flub anything herself.

At last the run-through was done and it was time to get ready for the real thing. Lisa found her stack of costumes and put on the one for the barnyard song. Once she was in it, there was really nothing to do but wait. Actually, there was one other thing she could do, and she did it. She peeped out at the audience. Like most theaters, the resort theater, an enormous open-air auditorium, had a peephole so that those backstage could observe the house before and during a performance. Lisa looked through the hole and was surprised at how many people she saw. The place was practically full! Almost everyone staying at the resort must have been there for the show. Would there be enough seats? Would Tec have to stand?

She squinted. Yes, there were her parents, happily looking for seats up at the front of the auditorium. There was no sign of Tec, but she suspected that he and the other kids in the group would be sitting more toward the back, and it was very hard to see that far, especially since the lights were dim back there. Lisa didn't have a chance of recognizing Tec from this distance, dimples notwithstanding.

And then it was time. The lights went out on the audience and on the stage.

Jane went out, bowed for the applause, and announced the beginning of the talent show. The audience applauded again. The curtain went up.

The first skit was the barnyard song. Everybody laughed and applauded. They were particularly fond of the cow and the horse, and they loved it when the rear end of the horse went in a different direction from the front end.

That was one of the things about an informal talent show like this. Flubs would happen, and the audience would enjoy them. The audience liked the undersea skit, too, and laughed hard when the fish complained about how silly the visitors looked with their masks and snorkels. There were a couple of jokes about string bikinis that Lisa thought would hit home to at least one group in the audience!

It was no surprise to Lisa that the audience loved the juggler. He was very good and had a funny patter to go along with his act. He was followed by the pianist, who played an amazing piece by Chopin, followed by some ragtime by Scott Joplin. Lisa would have liked to have watched that, but it was time for her to put on her Annie dress. She could hear the final strains of the rag and the wild applause of the audience.

It wasn't going to be easy to follow an act like that, but it was her turn. She felt every bit of churning in her stomach that she'd ever felt before a performance. It was worse than opening night for *Annie*. Lisa knew exactly what the difference was. Tec hadn't been there that time. But he was out there now.

She took a deep breath and walked out onstage, waiting for her cue.

Jane announced her as "Miss Lisa Atwood, San Felipe's own Annie!"

The curtain rose and the spotlight came on.

Jane played the introduction on the piano.

Lisa's mind became a total blank. Suddenly she didn't know where she was, she didn't know who she was, she had no idea what she was supposed to do, and she certainly didn't know any words to say or tune to sing.

And then the introduction was finished. She opened her mouth.

"The sun'll come out tomorrow!" she began automatically.

It was all there, every word, every note, every gesture. There wasn't a sound or a motion from the audience. They were stunned. Lisa's eyes glanced past her parents, sitting so far forward that the stage lights illuminated them. Her mother's eyes were filled with tears of pride. Her father just grinned.

And farther back in the audience . . . Well, she couldn't see Tec, but he could sure see her. Everybody in the room could see her. She knew it and she felt it. If there was one thing she'd learned performing, it was that a singer could tell when she held the audience. And she was holding them. They were even quieter for her than they had been for the piano player.

". . . a day awaaaaaaaaaaaaaaaaaaay!" she sang.

There were two seconds of quiet and then the audience broke into wild applause. Some people stood up. Some stomped their feet. Lisa's parents stood up, and her father shouted, "Bravo!" That was the kind of thing fathers were supposed to do, and Lisa was thrilled. She'd done an amazing job, and everybody in the audience thought she'd been singing for them. They were all wrong—except for one person. That performance had been for Tec. It was a performance he wouldn't easily forget!

Lisa could barely wipe the grin off her face as she headed backstage, rushing to her final costume change for the evening's grand finale.

It was all a blur and none of it seemed to matter very much after her solo, but it had to be done. She joined the rest of the kick line and they worked their way out onto the stage for a rousing rendition of "There's No Business Like Show Business." The audience clapped along with the music, which continued until Lisa thought she couldn't kick one more time. And then they clapped some more and the kick line kicked some more.

"Wonderful! You were all *wonderful*!" Jane congratulated the cast. She gave Lisa an extra-big hug. "Great job! Now go get changed and get ready for the party!"

The party. Lisa had almost forgotten about that. She needed to go visit with her parents, then find Tec and invite him to the cast party. He'd love it, she was sure.

Her parents were waiting by the stage door. They gave her giant hugs. Her mother was still crying and her father was still grinning, and both those things still made her feel good. She hugged them back, but her eyes were scanning the crowd over their shoulders, looking for Tec. She didn't see him.

Her parents said they were meeting up with their bridge friends, and if Lisa wanted to join them . . .

She explained about the cast party and told her parents she'd probably see them in the morning.

"Of course you will," said her father. "And pretty early, too. Our bus to the airport leaves at nine-thirty."

With that, they gave her a final hug and headed out to meet their friends. Her father's words hung heavily. It reminded Lisa that the whole wonderful week was almost over. It was hard to believe and something she didn't want to think about. And she didn't have to think about it right then. First, she'd think about the cast party.

She wandered through the milling crowd, hoping to find Tec. All around her people were shaking her hand, patting her back, and even giving her hugs.

"Mildred, we'll be able to say we heard this girl perform before she was famous," one man told his wife, who shook her hand vigorously.

"Thank you," Lisa said. She didn't actually think she was going to be famous enough for anyone to boast about, but it was sweet of him to put it that way.

"You were great!"

"Nice job!"

"Thanks for a terrific performance," came the accolades. Lisa answered each one and thanked them all.

Where was Tec?

Finally she was at the back of the auditorium, and there was still no sign of him. She followed the crowd, which was dispersing toward the lounge.

And there he was, sitting pretty much where he had been the last time she'd seen him.

"Hi there!" he greeted her warmly. "Where have you been?"

It stopped her cold. Was he kidding? He must be kidding.

"Right, like you didn't see it," she teased.

155

"What?" he asked, genuine confusion on his face.

Lisa was getting the idea that he wasn't kidding. "The talent show," she said. "Weren't you there?"

An elderly couple interrupted them. "You were marvelous!" the husband said to Lisa. "Just great!" the wife added. Lisa barely nodded.

"It was tonight?" Tec asked.

Lisa nodded.

"Oh boy," he said. But it wasn't enough to take away the terrible feeling crushing Lisa's heart.

The other kids in the group were beginning to wonder what was going on, and there was no way Lisa wanted to be there for one second more. "I've got to go," she said. "There's a cast party."

"See you later," Tec said. "And I'm sorry. I guess I blew it, huh?"

Lisa didn't answer. She just ran back to the comfort of her friends backstage.

An hour later, Lisa was feeling a little better. In spite of her anger and hurt, the party was fun, and she was glad she'd chosen that for her escape. The juggler had showed everybody how to juggle, working with props. Lisa didn't think she'd exactly mastered the skill. She had laughed, however, and that mattered because the simple act of laughing improved her mood.

She also ate, talked, received compliments and gave

them. It had been an exciting night, and she was totally accepted by all the adults as an equal. Lisa was proud of the whole show, and she was proud of what she'd done. The edge of her anger softened with the fun of the party and the crowd.

By midnight the party was breaking up. Lisa knew she had some packing to do before morning, though she didn't think it would take her long. She still wasn't ready to go back to her room. She had to do some thinking, and her room was not the place for it.

She headed for the beach. Once again, as it seemed was always the case on San Felipe, the moon was shining brightly and the stars were sparkling overhead. She walked along the edge of the water as she'd done so many of the previous nights, holding hands with Tec. How could he have missed the show? She'd told him about it enough times. He certainly knew she was in it. She'd been to so many rehearsals, and he knew every time. He also knew she was leaving the next day, didn't he? Could he have forgotten? Could the slow pace of the tropical days and nights have confused him about what day it was and when things happened? Could he possibly have misunderstood what she'd meant when she told him she had something special for him and when she'd reminded him about the show? How could that be?

She had to admit that she had never really told him outright that she had a solo, and she'd never told him directly that she'd planned to sing to him and for him. She took a deep breath of the fresh tropical night air. It seemed to clarify everything. It wasn't really Tec's fault. He hadn't meant to hurt her. He just didn't realize how much this had mattered to her, and there were a dozen ways she could have made it clearer to him. So much went on at a place like this resort that it was easy for someone to lose track of time. That must be it. He just didn't know when the show had been on, much less over.

She'd overreacted. It was the way it was with her mother, always flying off the handle about something that wasn't worth getting upset about. How could she do that? No wonder Tec had given her that weird look. She'd been overreacting to a little mistake he'd made, and it might have cost them their whole relationship.

She couldn't let that happen. She couldn't leave the resort with Tec still confused about what she felt for him. That could be the worst mistake of her life. He was crazy about her—as crazy about her as she was about him. She must have nearly broken his heart by being so upset. She had to fix things, and there was no time to waste.

Lisa picked up her sandals and ran along the beach,

hurrying to get back to the lounge, where she hoped she would find him.

She was running so fast that she almost didn't see the couple standing in the surf about twenty yards in front of her.

She paused, not wanting to embarrass them by running past them. Then they looked in her direction, toward the moon. It was Tec. And Shelley.

He must have come looking for me and Shelley came along to help, Lisa thought for a fleeting moment. She waved to them.

They didn't see her. In fact, they never saw her. Because at that moment, they turned to each other and kissed passionately. Shelley melted into Tec's arms as he drew the slender girl to him.

Lisa stopped, ducked into the shadows, and ran back to her cabin.

14

"HE KISSED THAT skinny little thing right in front of you?" Stevie wailed to Lisa as she finished telling her two best friends absolutely everything that had happened on San Felipe. They were having a sleepover at Stevie's house, and it seemed there was an awful lot to catch up on.

"I don't think Tec ever saw me that night on the beach," Lisa said.

"It doesn't matter. He shouldn't have been kissing anyone else, whether you saw him or not," Carole said.

"Wait'll I get my hands on that guy," Stevie said. "I'll punch his lights out."

"I'll fill his dimples in!" Carole added.

Lisa laughed. "You guys are the greatest," she said.

"You really know how to make me feel good. Without you, I got totally taken in by a real rat!"

"We aren't great enough to have been there when you needed us the most," said Stevie.

"Well, you would have set me straight early on, wouldn't you?" Lisa asked.

"The minute he forgot to meet you to go riding," Carole said. "That was a sure sign that he was a rat."

"Almost as bad as when he couldn't remember your last name, even after he'd kissed you," Stevie said.

"And when he forgot to go riding the second time," Carole said. "Bad sign, for sure."

"And then when he skipped out on the auditions and rehearsals," said Stevie.

"But then when he didn't stand up to Kiki about the smell of horses," Carole said, "I'd have known he was nothing but bad news."

"You two know everything!" Lisa said. "I wish you'd been there, but even here, you're making me feel a whole lot better."

"That's what friends are for," Stevie said, fluffing her pillow and reaching for another chocolate chip cookie.

"And while you should have been down there, saving my heart, I should have been up here, painting." Lisa poured herself a glass of milk.

"We did okay without you," Stevie said.

"Sure you did, and I knew you would. I just feel like I let you down."

"You didn't," said Carole. "You didn't have a choice." She chewed on a cookie thoughtfully.

"Unlike a certain P. Marsten," said Stevie.

"Maybe the only good males in this world are stallions," said Lisa.

"And geldings?" Carole asked. Starlight was a gelding.

"Definitely. Any horse, actually—male, female, or neutered."

"Okay, so if I've got this straight, what we've just agreed to is that the only good men are horses, right?" Stevie asked.

"Something like that," Carole agreed.

"Sounds good to me," Lisa said. "Oh, can we add Max to that?"

"Sometimes," Stevie said. "Like today."

"He was really surprised with all the work we'd done, wasn't he?" Carole asked.

"Knocked his socks off," Stevie said proudly.

"And he didn't believe Veronica for one half of one nanosecond when she tried to tell him she'd helped," said Carole.

"He's no fool," Lisa reminded them.

"Okay, we can add Max," Stevie conceded. "But that's the limit."

There was a knock on Stevie's door. It was Mrs. Lake. She asked Stevie to open the door for her because she couldn't manage it with her hands full.

"Of what?" Stevie asked, moving over to the door.

"Open the door and I'll show you," she said. There was a funny, happy sound to her voice.

Stevie opened the door. Her mother stood there with a very large arrangement of flowers, which she had to hold in both hands.

"The florist just delivered this," she said. "It's for you."

"Me?" Stevie asked as if there were any other daughter of hers in the room at that moment.

"You," Mrs. Lake confirmed.

Carole took the flowers. Stevie went for the card. She pulled the little greeting out of the very small envelope and read it.

"Okay, guys, we've got a problem," she said.

"What's that?" Carole asked, placing the flowers on Stevie's desk.

"The flowers are from Phil," Stevie told her friends.

"That's a problem?" Lisa asked.

"Well, here's what the card says: 'Stevie, I hope you can forgive me for letting you down about the painting.

163

I was being foolish and selfish. You are far more important to me than some old skiing trip. Any day. Love, Phil.' "

"What's the problem?" Carole asked.

Stevie grinned. "It means I'm going to have to ask you if we can include Phil on that list."

Lisa and Carole exchanged glances. Lisa shrugged.

"Okay," said Carole. "That means that the only good men are all horses, Max, and Phil."

"That's enough," said Stevie.

"For now," said Lisa.

ABOUT THE AUTHOR

BONNIE BRYANT is the author of more than a hundred books about horses, including The Saddle Club series, The Saddle Club Super Editions, the Pony Tails series, and Pine Hollow, which follows the Saddle Club girls into their teens. She has also written novels and movie novelizations under her married name, B. B. Hiller.

Ms. Bryant began writing The Saddle Club in 1986. Although she had done some riding before that, she intensified her studies then and found herself learning right along with her characters Stevie, Carole, and Lisa. She claims that they are all much better riders than she is.

Ms. Bryant was born and raised in New York City. She still lives there, in Greenwich Village, with her two sons.

Don't miss the next exciting
Saddle Club adventure . . .

HORSE
SPY
Saddle Club #94

When Carole Hanson learns that the newly elected president of a Middle Eastern country will be visiting Washington with his horse-crazy daughter, it seems only natural to write the girl a letter inviting her to come for a ride at Pine Hollow. Carole thinks she might get a reply with an interesting stamp on it. Instead of a stamp, however, Carole gets men with dark suits and sunglasses who walk around Pine Hollow talking into their lapels, looking for spies in the hayloft, and asking for security clearance for horses. Isn't this a little extreme? Especially since the four girls only wanted to go on a trail ride!

But when a real spy turns up at Pine Hollow, The Saddle Club rides to the rescue to protect national horse safety!

MEET
the SADDLE CLUB

Horse lover CAROLE . . .
Practical joker STEVIE . . .
Straight-A LISA . . .

THE SADDLE CLUB SUPER EDITIONS

THE SADDLE CLUB SPECIAL EDITIONS